The Lawman

Red Ridge Chronicles Book 3

Sarah Lamb

Copyright © 2025 Sarah Lamb

All rights reserved.

No portion of this book may be reproduced in any form without written permission from the publisher or author, except as permitted by U.S. copyright law.

This is a work of fiction. Names, characters, businesses, places, events, locales, and incidents are either the products of the author's imagination or used in a fictitious manner. Any resemblance to actual persons, living or dead, or actual events is purely coincidental.

A thank you to my proofreader, Brooke, and all of the lovely women who help ARC read to catch those typos I miss!

This book was not written by AI. Any typos are proudly (and embarrassingly!) my own human created ones!

This book is not allowed to be used in training AI.

Paperback ISBN: 978-1-960418-39-5
Large print ISBN: 978-1-960418-40-1

Contents

		V
1.	Chapter 1	1
2.	Chapter 2	9
3.	Chapter 3	17
4.	Chapter 4	23
5.	Chapter 5	31
6.	Chapter 6	37
7.	Chapter 7	45
8.	Chapter 8	55
9.	Chapter 9	63
10.	Chapter 10	71
11.	Chapter 11	79

12.	Chapter 12	85
13.	Chapter 13	93
14.	Chapter 14	99
15.	Chapter 15	105
16.	Chapter 16	111
17.	Chapter 17	119
18.	Chapter 18	129
19.	Chapter 19	137
20.	Chapter 20	143
21.	Epilogue	153
22.	What's next?	157
23.	Read all the Red Ridge Chronicles Books	159
24.	Note from Author	161
About Author		162

To each of the special people who have helped me bring this series and many of my other books to life: Brooke, for her on point suggestions and proofreading; Nancy, for her fantastic covers; Spencer, for his incredible narration; and you, dear readers, for your endless support. It takes a village, and I'd be lost without mine.

Chapter 1

1880s Red Ridge, Oregon

It was feeling a little lonely. Gavin Jefferson held in a sigh as he saddled his horse and glanced around his property.

How had this happened? First Eli...then Billy. He didn't blame either of them. They hadn't gone looking for love, but it sure had found them. And then changed all of their lives quicker than he could draw his revolver.

And no one was faster on the draw than him. Not even Eli.

Billy Madison had been married now almost a week to Mirabelle Blackstone, the pastor's daughter. Gavin and Eli Jones, Billy's best friends and fellow gunslingers, had worked hard alongside a few other men to build the newlyweds a house that was on the fifty acres Billy had bought.

The land bordered Gavin's and Eli's, and so they combined it, planning to continue their ranching venture together, and Billy's house was in sight, but that didn't stop the empty feeling inside Gavin right now. At night, when the windows glowed from lantern light, it almost made him feel worse, which was strange, because Gavin had never minded being alone. Not until recently.

It had been a long week. Mirabelle had insisted that he come for dinner whenever he wanted, and had made him eat with them twice this week. Hannah, Eli's wife, had done the same. But Gavin didn't like it.

Being there with the happy couples just reminded him of what he didn't have, what he couldn't have. He felt like an unnecessary wheel. A wagon didn't need five of them on the ground, when four did the moving just fine.

It hadn't mattered so much when Eli married. Gavin still had Billy. Now, he couldn't shake that feeling that he was intruding, somehow. His friends would be hurt if they knew he felt that way, and if he were truthful, Gavin knew that he wasn't intruding at all. He was welcomed. One of them. Family.

But that still didn't shake the lonely feeling he had. It wasn't something he'd be rid of anytime soon, either.

Now that Gavin was sheriff, things hadn't changed much from when he was a gunslinger, other than there were more rules. He had to do things by the law, even if that meant things went slower than he'd have liked, or differently altogether. Gone were the days of jumping on his horse, and using either his reputation or his gun to stop trouble. Now, there was paperwork. Judges. A reputation as a lawman, not a lawless man.

There was one thing, however, that hadn't changed. And that was it would be dangerous for him to have a woman of his own.

Sure, a few sheriffs did it, and Red Ridge had been fairly quiet. No one would blink if he found a woman who wanted to take a chance on a man like him. Anything that came up, he, Eli, and Billy dealt with quickly, but that didn't change the fact he still had an unpredictable and hazardous job, and a wife and later any children could be put in danger. His life could be at risk too, with the distraction of them at home or if someone were to know about them and try to use them against him.

But could he ever marry? Should he even entertain the idea? Gavin glanced down at the letter he'd gotten today. An old gunslinger friend by the name of James Clark had written him. Turned out he'd settled down in Kansas, after answering an ad for a woman needing a little help, much the same as Eli had.

James was doing well, loved his wife Grace, and they had three kids now, her two and one of their own on the way, though he considered all three his.

Would he ever get that? Gavin didn't have to think twice about the fact it might be nice to come home to a family. He saw how happy it had made Eli. How Billy was embracing each moment.

But facts were facts. He didn't have his eye on anyone, and there weren't too many women around here. It was better to keep to himself. Let his friends have their happiness. He'd be the responsible one. The one with his head on straight. Everyone knew a gunslinger couldn't settle.

Though Gavin might be wearing a badge and playing by the rules right now, deep inside, he was still a gunslinger. And gunslingers and women didn't mix. There was a reason men like him were often on the fringes of society. A necessary evil. And all that history didn't get erased just because a man put on a badge.

Gavin shoved the letter from James into his pocket. It was time to head to work. He double-checked his mare's saddle and grunted as he pulled the strap tighter. The mare liked to puff out her belly, and he didn't want to slide off. It wouldn't be a dignified look for either a gunslinger or a lawman to be riding on a crooked saddle.

So far, his time as sheriff hadn't been too bad. Overall, Red Ridge was quiet. Calm. That meant he didn't have to be there in town every moment. He could still oversee the ranching business with Eli and Billy. Though not as lucrative as their former occupation, he enjoyed it well enough.

Living right outside of town helped too, with not feeling trapped by too many people. It wasn't but a short ride to his office, but it was enough that he got to enjoy the quiet, and keep an eye on things as he rode past.

Gavin dropped his mare at the livery and started making his rounds. It was a fine day out, and though it would be hours before noon, the sun was heating things up. The town was starting to bustle. Wagons came and went, and small groups of people clustered together talking.

"Morning, Sheriff," a voice called.

Gavin turned and found himself face to face with old Gus, the foreman at Eli and Hannah's place. Gus was like family to them all. He'd been Hannah's protector before Eli came.

"Morning, Gus," Gavin said. "Looks to be a fine day."

Gus nodded. "It will be. No twinges in my knee."

"Good. What about tomorrow?" Gavin asked.

The old ranch hand nodded, pointing to his leg. "Storm in the afternoon. Won't last long."

"Thanks." Gavin nodded. Some of the others gave the old man a hard time about his weather knee, but Gavin had never known him to be wrong. He never knew when the information might come in handy too, so he always asked.

He glanced around the town, his eyes seeking out any signs of upset. However, all seemed well. As usual.

"What are you doing in town today?" Gavin asked as his eyes landed back on Gus. "Care to get something at the diner with me?"

"Came for a few things at Mrs. Stover's shop," Gus answered. As he said her name, he smoothed his wrinkled shirt. "I've got to hurry back. Eli needs nails, but next time. They've got good pies."

"Sure do," Gavin agreed. "When you go back, give Meg and Benjamin a hug from me. Tell Meg to make her Uncle Billy some of those cookies he likes so much."

"I will," Gus promised. Then, his creased face grew serious, and his eyes squinted. "How you holding up? Being the last man to settle down."

"I'm fine," Gavin said, crossing his arms over his chest. "I like quiet. You know that."

It wasn't a lie. He did enjoy it, even if as of late the quiet was getting a little too loud.

"Maybe you need to find yourself a woman." Gus squinted at him again and shook his head. "You'll want one with a little fire. Someone to keep you on your toes. Redheads are good for that."

Gavin laughed. "Oh? Well, maybe you need one yourself."

Tucking his thumbs into his belt, Gus rose on his toes and rocked back. "I've got my eye on one, but she don't like younger men. Whelp, see you later, young feller. 'Bout to head to the barber, then stop in for the supplies."

"That where she works?" Gavin asked, letting his eyes drift toward the closest of the two general stores.

"Nuh-uh." Gus shook a wrinkled finger at him. "I'm not telling nothing about nothing."

Gavin laughed. "All right, old man. Get going. But before you do, you sure about the weather? I'm sensing something in the air." He glanced at the sky.

The stagecoach approached, and with it the typical cloud of dust. Townsfolk stepped back or turned their faces away to let it settle without choking.

"It's not the weather, my knee is just right," Gus said, then tipped his hat and left.

When he glanced back, the passengers on the stage alighted. A woman climbed out clutching a carpetbag, and Gavin tensed.

That right there was trouble, if ever he'd seen it.

Chapter 2

Winifred Anderson stepped out of the way, just barely, as a passenger from the stagecoach pushed her and then started running.

"Stop or I'll shoot!" a man, who she prayed was the sheriff and not a ruffian, shouted, as he bolted after the former passenger.

People stopped to stare, then two other men clustered with the first. One grabbed the man's arms, twisting them behind his back, while the other two stood with a hand on each side of him, and hauled the passenger toward the sheriff's office.

Winnie couldn't say that concerned her any. She'd had some suspicions about the man on their journey together. He never seemed to sleep and stared at each of them in turn. It was downright disconcerting.

Hopefully she'd have a chance to find out who he was and why he'd been captured, and he'd be sent away. At least the law in this town seemed on top of things.

She stooped and picked up her carpetbag that had fallen from her grip when she'd been shoved. Nerves filled her, and her stomach rolled and jolted. It was almost as though it had forgotten she'd stepped off the stage and had gotten used to the constant swaying of the last few days. Of course, she knew the real reason her stomach refused to calm itself.

Winnie was pretending to be someone else, and about to marry that woman's intended.

Gulping in a deep breath and resting her free hand on her stomach, she studied her surroundings, then headed toward the hotel. Red Ridge seemed to be a good-sized town. It had everything a body could need, and then some. There were two general stores, one larger than the other, a diner, butcher, bakery, sheriff's office, bank, hotel, post office, dressmaker, shoemaker, blacksmith... She shook her head in surprise. The further she walked, the more she saw.

It was a little exciting being here. Winnie had never traveled so far before on her own. Usually, she was in the capacity of her mistress's maid. This was rather exciting. And scary.

Though Claudette had told her there was no need to worry—and to not use her real name, Winifred—Winnie still felt nervous. However, the opportunity was too good to let slip through her fingers.

As she pushed open the door, Winnie glanced about the large hotel lobby. A walnut desk was sitting near the back room by a staircase, and she started toward it.

"May I help you?" a man asked.

"Yes. Win—Claudette McMillin. I've a room reserved?"

He looked down and thumbed through a book. "Yes, Miss McMillin. I'll send someone to carry your luggage."

"This is all I have," she said quietly. "I'll manage fine, thank you."

"Very well," the man answered. "I'm the desk manager. Should you have any questions, please come find me." He slid her a room key and pointed down a hallway. "Your room is three doors down on the left."

"Thank you," Winnie said, and made her way to the room.

Once Winnie had unlocked the door, she stared in appreciation. No doubt Claudette would have sniffed and asked why the accommodations were so poor, but Winnie thought they were lovely.

Though she'd traveled many places in her capacity as maid or companion, including out West twice, it never ceased to amaze her that, for people who didn't have the ease of getting goods like they did in the East, they still had fine buildings, furnishings, and decorations.

This room was no exception. The room, though small, looked comfortable. A rich red and white quilt rested atop the bed, with a beautiful mountain pieced into it. A mirror hung overtop the washbasin, and there was a chest of drawers, a small table and chair, and a window that overlooked a small garden.

It was all she needed to be comfortable. Winnie pulled forth her watch, a gift from Claudette, and checked the time. She had less than a half hour before she was to meet the man she was to marry in the hotel lobby.

Hurriedly, she changed her dress and set about removing as much dust as she could from her face and hands in the basin. Once she felt refreshed, Winnie dressed in a green dress, and fixed her hair. She felt much better and looked much better, but...would Mr. Rudolph Duncan accept her?

Winnie left her room and slowly walked to the lobby. Nerves filled every inch of her now. This was a bad idea, and she didn't know why she'd ever let Claudette talk her into it.

No. Wait, she knew.

It was because Claudette always got what she wanted. This being no exception.

Winnie wondered where Claudette was now. Off somewhere wonderful, likely. When she eloped, she'd been full of giggles and daydreams, talking about the places her beau was going to take her.

"Miss McMillin?" A man much older than her stood, squinting slightly.

"Y-yes," she answered, moving closer. Then asked, "Mr. Duncan?"

"Yes. I've reserved us a table in the restaurant. Let's get a bite, shall we? Stage food is not always appealing, I know." He smiled at her, but it didn't quite meet his eyes.

"That was most kind of you," Winnie said, taking his offered arm.

So far, this was going well. Perhaps she could pull this off.

Winnie waited as Mr. Duncan pulled out her chair and they sat.

"Order whatever you like," the man said. Then, he looked at her again. "Forgive me for staring. It's just...you don't look at all like you did the last two times I met you. Nor do you look like your recent photograph."

Winnie's heart nearly stopped. Claudette and Mr. Duncan had met before? How in the world could Claudette have left that out? And why didn't she tell her? Why did she send Winnie here into this frightful mess, knowing that she'd never be able to pull this off?

Claudette was selfish. She knew this. But even this was a new low. It was all Winnie could do to keep her hands from shaking.

"No matter," he said, "let's order."

She nodded, and let him choose. Before long, slices of ham, fried potatoes, green beans, and cornbread sat before her. Winnie was famished, but it was hard to eat. Fear raced through her every nerve.

They ate in near silence, and then Mr. Duncan leaned back in his chair and sighed. "Young woman," he started.

Winnie thought she might faint at his expression. She felt sick and wished she'd not eaten as much as she had.

Mr. Duncan continued, "I don't know who you are, but I know you aren't Claudette McMillin. I've known Claudette since she was knee high. Her father and I are good friends."

When Winnie opened her mouth to protest or to say something, anything, to forestall him, he held up a hand to stop her. "However, I do know that Claudette is very opinionated and doesn't like being told what to do. I suspect she put you up to this, and I also suspect her father has no idea what she's up to."

Winnie looked down, and a tear rolled down her cheek. "It's true," she whispered. "She told me to come in her place. I'm her—I was her maid."

"I see. That doesn't surprise me." Mr. Duncan rose. "I'm afraid that my marriage contract was between myself and Claudette. Not you. While I'm sure that you are a fine young woman, the fact remains that I was promised a McMillin woman as my bride. Not a..." He waved his hand.

"Anderson. Winifred Anderson," she whispered.

"An Anderson," he finished. Sympathy filled his face, and he sighed. "I'm sorry. But I can't marry you in trade. Her father and I were to do business, and she was part of the deal. You understand. I'm going to send him a message."

He set some money down on the table. "That will cover our meal. Your room is already paid in full for the week, but that's all I am willing to do. You'll have to make your own arrangements for meals and transportation back home."

"No!" Winnie gasped as she stood. "Please! I-I'll do anything."

But he didn't stop as he left. Winnie gathered her skirts and rushed after him. Mr. Duncan walked through the lobby, and she followed him, humiliated by her pleading in such a public place. There was no help for it, though. "Please," she begged. "You don't understand."

"I might not," he agreed, "but I won't be made a fool of. Good day."

He walked away without looking back at her. Winnie squeezed her hands into fists. Fury filled her. She was angry.

Angry at Claudette, first and foremost, but then angry at herself, now more than ever. She'd agreed to this foolish plan, and now she—and those dearest to her—were paying for her stupidity.

With little to her name, in an unfamiliar town, unable to marry a man of means to help her, and with her younger siblings in danger, how was she to rescue them?

Chapter 3

"I'm your best friend," Billy said stubbornly, his jaw jutting out. "And I'm taking it personally that you won't tell me what's wrong." He paused, and his eyes grew worried. "It's not because you miss me, is it?"

"Miss you? Couldn't wait to be rid of you." Gavin smirked. Then he sighed. "Look, it's…"

He stopped. How was he going to say what had been bothering him all night? Mirabelle had just about forced him over for dinner. He hadn't minded, but it just made him focus more on the thought that had been on his mind all afternoon.

"What's wrong with me?" Gavin suddenly asked.

"I could give you a list," Billy said, as he stretched out and kicked his heels up on the rail of Gavin's front porch.

They'd walked there after dinner, and he took his usual chair.

"But," Billy added, "I don't think that's what you mean."

Gavin sighed. "It's not. Today, when the stage pulled in, there was a wanted man on it."

"I heard," Billy groaned. "And I missed out."

"You aren't the only one who missed out on something," Gavin said. "There were several people on that stage, including an attractive woman. She seemed to stare right through me. Not at. Through. Used to be I couldn't go anywhere without fluttering eyelashes and giggles aimed my way. Now, look at me. I've turned respectable. I'm the sheriff. And sheriffs don't have fun or googly eyes headed their direction."

He slouched down in his chair and kicked at the floorboards. There was a loose nail, and he pushed at it.

"So that's what it is?" Billy asked. "Worried you're past your prime?"

"I'm no Gus," Gavin said. Then he groaned. "No, even Gus has someone he likes and who likes him. I'm not looking to settle, don't get that in your mind," he said, glaring at Billy, who raised his hands in surrender. "I'm just wondering what's happened all of a sudden and why I don't get the female attention I used to. I might not have wanted to settle, but made a man feel good he was wanted."

Billy shrugged. "Could be one or a dozen things," he said. "There's fewer women here who aren't married, and you don't leave town anymore, since you're the sheriff. Might also be they're too scared on account of your reputation to approach you."

Those were both good thoughts, and Gavin hadn't thought of either. Back in the days he roamed place to place, most folks didn't know who he was. There were no preconceived notions.

"Also," Billy continued, "could be that sourpuss face of yours, or the gray ha—Ouch! What'd you do that for?" Billy rubbed at his head and scowled.

"If I'd have meant for it to hurt, you'd be crying." Gavin smirked. Then he grew serious. "But you've got a point. On some of it, anyway. Not the grays. I don't have any."

They sat there quietly. The moon was rising and stars were coming out of hiding. For a short time, it felt familiar. Comfortable. Like before. But Gavin knew deep within him, things had changed. He was okay with that. Even wanted a little of that change for himself.

"Room for one more?"

"Always," Billy said, not even looking over at the newcomer.

Gavin nodded a hello as Eli took his place on the porch. "Didn't hear you ride up," he said.

"That's because I was walking. Just felt like it. Felt like I needed to be here." Eli glanced at Gavin. "I heard a little of what you said. Feeling like it's time to change something?"

"I don't know," Gavin sighed. "Never thought I'd say it, but maybe."

"Just because you settle down doesn't mean you stop being yourself," Eli told him.

Billy was nodding in agreement. "True."

"You know," Gavin said quietly. "You two got lucky, but that's not something I've ever had. Luck. I've had to work at everything I've ever done. What I have is skill. Effort. I feel like maybe that's the problem. I don't have luck. So even if I wanted to settle one day, doesn't mean the woman I want will just be there for me, like she was for you both."

Billy looked over. His eyes were serious. "So, put some effort in. If that's where you get your results, then that's where you get 'em."

"That's just it." Gavin shook his head. "If you've got to change yourself for someone to make them like you, is that even love?"

Eli sighed. "Don't know. I'm a gunslinger, through and through. That means not always doing things by the book."

"Sometimes, you've got to, not that you'd ever hear me telling the man with the badge that," Billy said.

"But that's my problem, isn't it?" Gavin said. "I pinned on this badge, and now I'm paying for it."

"Not by yourself," Eli told him. "We're here, and the day you've had enough, we'll send away for a replacement. Won't be as good, but I'd rather have my friend happy than feeling trapped."

Gavin didn't answer. He couldn't. There was a lump in his throat, so he did all he could do. He picked up his violin and started playing to the night sky, letting the melody express what he couldn't.

Chapter 4

It was pouring. Winnie knew she looked a mess as she went from place to place seeking work. But what else was there to do? She only had a few days paid for at the hotel and not enough money to continue it or get a stagecoach ticket home.

Not that she had a job back there, so what good would that do? There was nothing there. Not even her siblings. She only knew they were missing, possibly in danger, and now her chance of having the financial means to rescue them was gone.

She took a deep breath and pushed open the door to the smaller general store. This would be the eighth place she'd stopped in. Perhaps it would also be the one that offered her a position.

As she walked inside, Winnie desperately hoped she wasn't dripping on the floor. The store was clean and orderly. Everything was stacked neatly, from bolts of cloth to boxes of goods, and jars with everything from buttons and candy to spices and tea.

The store smelled heavenly as well, and it was dry. Winnie would have loved to linger had it not been for two things. First, she was looking for work, and second, she had little money to her name and right now, every penny was important.

An older woman behind the counter, and who she assumed was the store owner, smiled at her. "Hello, welcome. Dear, you look a tad soggy. Why don't you come closer to the stove?"

Winnie wouldn't disagree on either of those accounts, and she answered, "Thank you. I appreciate it."

Two women around her own age smiled and nodded at her. One asked, "Are you new here?"

"I-I..." Winnie took a deep breath. It wasn't like her at all to want to tell strangers what had happened to her. Was it the desperation urging her to speak?

"If there's some trouble," one of the women said, concern on her face, "perhaps we can help. I'm Hannah. This is Mirabelle." She pointed to the other woman.

"And I'm Mrs. Stover," the store owner replied.

"I am seeking employment, urgently," Winnie answered. She twisted her hands together. "I came to wed a man, but I was…not what he expected. He broke the contract."

The contract that likely wasn't even valid. After all, she wasn't Claudette, who was the one whose name was on the contract. Not that she wanted to explain that part. No, better to let others think it was just an unsuitable pairing.

"Oh my," Mirabelle said, bringing her hands to her mouth. "That's terrible."

"My dear, why don't you go and speak to the sheriff?" Mrs. Stover said. "Perhaps he can advise you. It could be there is some recourse you could take, financially, to at least help you get back home. Surely the man must be responsible if he's broken your agreement."

"That's right." Hannah nodded. "In the meantime, I know over at the diner they are looking for another pair of hands to help out. Have you tried there?"

"I have not," Winnie said. "I will do so."

"Make sure you do," Mirabelle said. "Tell them we sent you. The sheriff as well."

Winnie nodded and turned away from the warmth of the stove. She was grateful that it had helped dry her out. Not only did she feel warmer, but she was more hopeful. Even if her help wasn't needed here, perhaps she could find something at the diner. The sheriff, though…she still wasn't sure if she should even step foot in there.

After all, truthfully, she was the one at fault. She'd been pretending to be Claudette. It didn't matter that the other woman had been convinced no one would be the wiser to their plan. It also didn't matter that the reason was desperation. The sheriff wasn't going to help her.

Unless...him being sheriff, perhaps he could just advise her in general. She didn't know anything about contracts. If it was true that perhaps she could be owed some sort of financial assistance, that would be very helpful. She really didn't know what to do, and had almost nothing to her name.

Also, Winnie had the feeling if she didn't speak to the sheriff, then Hannah might go to him herself, and then she'd be in real trouble, especially if the sheriff wanted to investigate. If she went herself, she could control what was said.

"Thank you, all of you," Winnie said, and smiled her gratitude. "I'll do that right now."

When she pushed through the door outside, she was grateful to see that the rain had lightened. Perhaps that was a good sign.

Stepping on the sidewalk, she went the short distance to the sheriff's office, and hesitated. The other women had seemed so sure she should go there, but they also didn't know the whole story. Maybe she should leave.

But the moment Winnie thought that, there was a loud clap of thunder that rattled her teeth, and the skies opened up angrily. Gasping, she pushed the sheriff's door open, seeking shelter.

There wasn't much light streaming in from the window, what with the sky being all cloudy. A lamp was lit, but it was low and on an unoccupied desk. Perhaps he wasn't here. She should go. Try the diner, and come back later. Or not.

"Hello."

Winnie startled at the voice. She hadn't seen anyone. As she turned her head, she saw the desk and the man standing behind it. He had cool eyes, dark hair, and sent a shiver up and down her spine. It was almost as though he were staring right through her.

"Hello, I'm looking for the sheriff," Winnie said a little nervously.

"You've found him," the man answered, coming closer.

He looked her over carefully, from the top of her damp hair to her boots that had mud on them. Winnie flushed. She looked a fright, she knew it.

"How can I help?" he asked, and pointed to a chair.

"Oh. I should stand. I'm afraid I got caught in the rain," Winnie apologized.

"It's just water. It'll dry," the man said. "Sheriff Gavin Jefferson."

"Winifred Anderson," she answered. "But everyone calls me Winnie."

He nodded and motioned to the chair again, and turned to his desk. This time, she sat. If she did, she could hopefully hide any nervous fidgeting that she might do.

"I was over at the general store," she started. "The owner, a Mrs. Stover, and two women, Hannah and Mirabelle, said I should come."

He nodded. "Go on."

"Well, I...I came here to be married," she said.

"Congratulations."

"They aren't in order," she said quietly. "The man didn't marry me."

He looked surprised at that. "Why not?"

"I wasn't who he thought I was," she answered.

There. That told the situation, but didn't paint her in too bad of a light, did it? She offered a smile, trying hard to do the ones she'd seen Claudette do so often, ones that melted the hard gazes of men into concern or sappy smiles.

But this man was different. His eyes hardened, and he set his hands on the top of his desk, fingers laced.

"Miss Anderson," he said, "there's a lot you aren't telling me. I can't help you unless you tell me everything. Even if you do, I'll be honest, I might not be able to help you. But I can promise that withholding information or lying isn't going to help whatever situation you are in."

Why hadn't the look worked? She'd practiced it so often. Her voice was faint. She wondered if he could hear it over the thumping of her heart. "What makes you think I'm withholding anything?"

"Because I've been a gunslinger most of my life. The sheriff job is new, but my instincts are still the same. I can spot discomfort, half truths, and trouble a mile away. Red Ridge is a quiet town. My friends and I keep it that way. Hannah and Mirabelle are married to my friends. My gunslinger friends."

"Oh." Winnie gulped. What in the world had she gotten herself into?

"Have you brought trouble, or are you running from it?" the sheriff asked.

That made Winnie think. Which had she done? Neither really. But how could she tell him that? Truthfully, the man was a little scary. Should she answer? Or would running be a better option?

"I'm waiting, Miss Anderson," he said.

Chapter 5

Gavin watched closely as a range of emotions flashed over Miss Anderson's face at his question. It had unsettled her. But what he saw, fear, hurt, desperation...it proved that the quiet last few weeks were about to get interesting.

He waited patiently. That was often one of the strongest moves a man could make. Act like you had all the time in the world. Let the criminal—or in this case, strange woman—feel the weight of your gaze. The many options you had before you, when they had none.

It was a powerful thing to do. Not one to be overused, but a tool in the belt, much like his guns were.

Miss Anderson opened and closed her mouth, and he watched as that wave of indecision crashed over her. Was what she was about to say so terrible she couldn't even speak? Or was she forming a lie?

"It seemed like a good idea at the time," she blurted out.

"What did?" Finally. They were getting somewhere.

"I agreed to get married. A contract was signed, and I showed up here. But he...didn't want me? And so I am here, without any money and I'm looking for a job and—"

Her words were too fast. Getting jumbled. Something was missing. Gavin held up a hand. "Stop. I can't help you when I can't understand you. Start from the beginning. You signed a contract."

"Well, no. Not me. The person I worked for." She seemed nervous. Her hands were squeezing together, just like his head was starting to. The dull ache was spreading from his eyes to his temples.

"Who did you work for? And why did they sign the contract instead of you?" It was all he could do to stay calm. Irritation was filling him.

Miss Anderson suddenly stilled. "I don't know if I can tell you."

He smacked the desk. "Then why did you come here? Why are you wasting my time?"

To his surprise, she didn't startle. In fact, she raised her voice and shouted, "I don't know! Maybe because I have nowhere else to go and no one to help me and those women told me to!"

He blew out a breath. "I'm sorry. It's just—"

"I'm not making sense," she finished, quieter now. "I'm sorry." Miss Anderson closed her eyes, drew in a deep breath, and squared her shoulders. "Right. From the beginning. I'm Winifred Anderson. I was employed by a young woman to be her maid and companion. She was quite well off, as you can imagine, to have a maid. Cla—She was to get married. Her father had arranged it some years prior, but when the time came, she refused to go."

Now they were getting somewhere.

"And so you went in her place?" Gavin leaned back, listening closely.

"I didn't want to." The woman sighed, and her shoulders slumped. "She pressed me, and I needed the money. She told me that if I went, my needs, and those of my siblings, would be provided for. However, what she neglected to tell me was that she'd met the man several times and that when I arrived, he would know right away that I wasn't her. We don't look a thing alike."

Gavin couldn't help but feel a little sympathetic. Sometimes rich folks did things like this, thought only of themselves, never paying any attention to the fact it might ruin the outcome for an average person, like Miss Anderson.

He could sense she was a good woman. One with a few secrets, but still good.

"I'm sorry," he said with a slow shake of his head. "It sure sounds to me like you were taken advantage of. What happened when you got here?"

Her eyes were honest as she answered. "He told me he knew I wasn't her, and would be contacting her father to find out where she was. He was generous and paid for my dinner and my room at the hotel the rest of the week. But I'm on my own after that." She dropped her gaze to her lap. "He was more than generous, if I'm being truthful. But I don't know what to do. If anything can be done."

"What do you want to do?" Gavin asked. "Are you just wanting your fare back home?"

She shook her head. "No. That's useless to me. I came here because I needed to marry him, to have the security and the financial means to legally adopt my younger siblings."

That hadn't been what he'd expected her to say. Gavin let his gaze roam around the room. What could he say that wouldn't make her situation worse?

"Just tell me the truth," she said quietly. "Please. Is there anything I can do?"

"You might not like it," he answered honestly. "The contract you had wasn't between you and that man. He is within his legal right to take you before the judge for trying to swindle him."

At her gasp, he nodded. "That's right. I imagine you didn't think about that. Maybe the woman you worked for didn't either, but that's the sort of thing that could happen when impersonating a person, especially one well off."

Anger filled her eyes, and she hissed, "When I see her again..." but she didn't finish, and was fighting to clench her jaw. Her hands were balled into fists. He almost felt sorry for her. Perhaps he should feel more sorry for the woman who'd tricked her.

"It seems to me, whoever this man was at least was kind enough to not see you out in the street." Gavin frowned. "I'll send a note to a man I know who is our circuit judge. I won't mention your name, just ask for advice. But my instincts tell me he's legally not obligated to do a thing for you. I'm sorry."

"Don't be." She sighed. "I know it. I knew it from the start. I wish I'd never said yes."

"Why did you?" Gavin asked. "For the money?"

"Not just that," she answered. "But because without money, and being an unmarried woman, there's a lot I can't do in life. Especially in regards to helping my siblings."

Miss Anderson stood and held out her hand. He took it, instinctually, as she said, "Thank you, Sheriff. I apologize for wasting your time. I don't dare delay. I understand there might be a position open at the diner, and I'm hoping to acquire it."

Without looking back, she left, and Gavin leaned back in his chair, propped his feet on his desk, and watched her.

She'd gotten herself into a fine mess. But he had the feeling that she wasn't telling him the whole story. There was a lot that didn't add up. Like, why would someone let themselves be talked into pretending to be someone else? There had to be more than the money. More than needing to be married to adopt her siblings.

He didn't sense dishonesty in what she said. Not at all. Just it was incomplete. Gavin sighed, pulled his feet off his desk, and walked over to the window. The rain had stopped, and the sun was shining brightly, just like Gus had said it would. He just hoped for Miss Anderon's sake that things would look up for her too.

Chapter 6

When Winnie walked out, her head high and her shoulders back, she was grateful to see the rain had stopped. Sun was peeking through the clouds, and with any luck, that was a sign from above that the cloud hanging over her would lift as well.

She walked toward the diner, still in disbelief. She hadn't meant to tell all of her story. Just, the sheriff's gaze...it was so intense. So focused. Like he could see right inside of her.

Had he just been an ordinary man, she wouldn't have minded. She might have liked it, being the object of his attention. Beneath his slightly gruff exterior, she sensed a kind person who liked to help others. It had startled her to hear he had been a gunslinger. Still was a gunslinger? She wasn't sure. And those two women in the store were married to his friends? What would it be like to be married to a gunslinger?

She could hardly imagine it. Weren't gunslingers supposed to be dangerous? Rough? Ugly and scarred, dirty and, well, anything other than how he had seemed. Her thoughts drifted back toward Hannah and Mirabelle. They had been so nice, she wished she could stay here, become friends with them.

Back home, other than Claudette, she'd never had anyone really to talk to. The other servants were either men, and it was forbidden to talk with them, or else they were all much older than her. There was no one to confide in, though she'd dearly longed for it at times.

Of course, she'd been Claudette's confidante, that came with the job, but Claudette didn't care about listening to anyone but herself. Even if she had been willing, it wouldn't have been proper for her to share her own worries or secrets.

Like about her siblings. Once she found out if she had the job at the diner or not, she'd send a message to the detective she'd hired to track them down. It had been more than a month, and she'd not heard a thing from him. Winnie hoped everything was okay. Usually, he updated her every two weeks. She'd even paid him before she left for Red Ridge when she sent word she was traveling. This just wasn't like him.

THE LAWMAN 39

The diner appeared in front of her, shaking her from her thoughts. Winnie pushed open the door. The place was quite charming. Perhaps two dozen tables that could seat four were in neat rows. A few potted plants and paintings decorated the room. It was quite busy inside. Women were sipping tea, men were shoveling in food, and a tired-looking woman came from the back.

"Help you, love?" she asked wearily.

"I was told you might be hiring," Winnie said. Then, she quickly added, "Hannah and Mirabelle said so."

"You're hired. When can you start?" The woman glanced at her customers. "Now?"

"Ah, I'd be glad to," Winnie said, surprised the woman didn't ask if she'd ever done anything like this before or check to be sure she was trustworthy. Either she was incredibly desperate, or else the recommendation from Hannah and Mirabelle carried great value. Winnie tried to sound confident, though she'd never worked in any eating establishment before. "What would you like me to do?"

"Follow me," the woman said and headed to the kitchen. "I'm Madge Simpson. Call me Madge."

"Winifred Anderson. Call me Winnie," she replied.

"I had two girls quit the same day. Left to be mail-order brides. Never they mind what it would do to me. My cook, Lisa"—she pointed to another tired-looking woman—"and I are up to our ears. I don't have time to explain everything, but if you could plate the pies, set the rolls in baskets, and help with the dishes, that would be a wonderful start."

"Here's a spare apron," Lisa said.

Winnie grabbed it, rolled up her sleeves, and got to work. Under Lisa's direction, she cut each pie into eight wedges, put four rolls to a basket, and then set to washing a teetering pile of dishes.

Hours flew by, and she couldn't help but marvel at how Madge and Lisa kept going. They had to do this every day? That included cooking the food, waiting on the tables.

Finally, Madge said, "I'm locking the door. Let's have a bite."

Lisa fixed up plates with the leftover food—meatloaf, mashed potatoes, steamed carrots, fresh cucumbers, and rolls. "You take what pie you want too," she said, helping herself to a wedge of apple. "We eat once the customers are gone for dinner. We eat before they come for an early lunch."

"Leftovers from today are breakfast," Madge said, as she took her plate and went to a table in the kitchen, "so as long as you don't mind meals from here, you'll get three a day when you work."

Winnie followed her to the table. "I don't mind a bit. It smells wonderful." She took her first bite and said, "Lisa, you are a wonderful cook."

The other woman grinned, but didn't answer as she ate.

Madge let out a contented sigh. "My feet are aching. I'm glad you are here, Winnie. Just moved to the area?"

"Yes," Winnie said. "I thought I was going to marry, but it turned out not to be the case. I was not who he expected. Now, I'm stranded. I am so glad you've given me a job. I have some siblings I want to send for as soon as I have the money to pay for their fare."

"Aren't you a good sister," Madge said. "Well, I don't have a room you can use, but the boarding house is cheap. You can check there."

Winnie nodded. "Thank you, I will in the morning. I'm fortunate enough to have three more nights paid at the hotel."

"That's a nice place," Lisa said.

"Tell me about yourselves," Winnie said. "I'd love to know more about you two."

Lisa laughed. "There's not much to tell about me. I enjoy cooking; that's why I'm here. I'm the oldest child, and believe it or not, it's less chaotic around here than it is at home."

Winnie laughed along with her and Madge. What a funny idea that was.

"For myself," Madge said, "As you know, I run the diner. That doesn't leave me too much time for anything else."

"Neither of you are married?" Winnie asked. Then, she apologized, "I'm sorry, I don't mean to pry. It's just in the West..."

"Oh, we understand," Lisa said, shaking her head. "No, I'm not yet. I've my eye on a rancher. Maybe one day. We aren't ready yet."

"I thought I had someone," Madge said. "But he wanted me to give up the diner. Stay home and cook just for him. I couldn't do that. I watched my mother give up her dream, and when my father died, it was too late for her to capture it, and she had no financial means. That is in part why I started this diner. I don't want to be in that position, and it allows me to help her."

Winnie nodded. "I appreciate you sharing such confidences with me," she said. "Oddly enough, it makes me feel better about my own situation."

Giving her a small smile, Madge said, "Each of us has a challenge or struggle we are going through. That's why one of my rules here is to be kind. You never know when your kind words are just what someone needs, and when your words of frustration might be more fuel to the fire."

Lisa echoed her sentiments, and Winnie nodded in agreement. It was true. Guilt washed over her at the number of times she'd spoken carelessly because she was tired or frustrated and said something she hadn't intended. Hopefully, with Madge and Lisa's examples, she'd do better.

While they finished eating, Madge and Lisa explained how the diner ran and where they needed Winnie's help. For lunches, it would be to serve the food. For dinners, she'd split her time between the dining room and the kitchen.

If today was anything to go by, Winnie knew she'd be tired, but the work wasn't difficult, and it was a job.

As she left the diner and walked back to the hotel, she was full of yawns. Though she couldn't wait to climb into bed, she needed to send a letter to the detective.

This job, though it might not quite provide for all she needed, was a start. At least it would allow her to have most of her meals provided for, pay for a room, and cover the cost of the detective. She'd worry about the fee to adopt her siblings once they were found.

If only Mr. Duncan had thought she was Claudette. She could have gotten used to being called Claudette. Used to pretending. In a way, she had been since she left the orphanage. But that's what had gotten her into this mess.

Entering her hotel room, Winnie allowed herself the comfort of her nightdress, then sat down to write the detective a letter. Her pencil scrawling, she kept it brief, leaving out her worries that she'd not had any updates.

Winnie closed her eyes and pressed the letter to her heart. With all of her being, she hoped she'd get an answer. Something deep inside told her that her siblings were in danger, and she was desperate to rescue them.

Chapter 7

"What's that sour look for?" Billy asked. "Meg bring you by some cookies?"

Gavin couldn't stop his laugh. Ever since little Meg had learned to bake cookies, she loved to make them for her "uncles." Neither he nor Billy liked them, but it made her so happy to hear they loved them, they put up with it.

Gavin had a chipped back tooth to prove it.

"She did, actually," Gavin said with a smile. "But they were for you. Not me." He reached under his desk and pulled out a small package wrapped in brown paper.

Billy stared at it and swallowed hard. "You sure? I-I'll share."

"No, no! And hurt her feelings? Look! She even made a card," Gavin said, sliding over a piece of paper.

Slowly, Billy reached out and took the square of paper. "Uncle Billy," he read, "Uncle Gavin said he ate all yours on accident, so I'm making you more. Love, Meg."

He glared at Gavin, who laughed and held up his hands.

"I'll pay you back," he grumbled.

"Fine, fine. Just not with her cookies," Gavin smirked.

"She'll get better," Billy promised. "Eli said so."

"If she doesn't kill us first, I look forward to that day," Gavin agreed.

Billy sat across from him. "So, tell me. What's going on?"

Gavin shook his head. "Mirabelle tell you about the woman who came into the general store looking for work?"

"Yeah. She did. Something about a rejected mail-order bride?"

"Not quite." Gavin frowned, and tried to string his words together. It was difficult when he knew he didn't have all the facts. "She's leaving something out," he told his friend. "And that's what puzzles me. She told me part, that she'd near been forced or tricked into pretending that she was this man's intended. That she had no idea the man had known the woman she was supposed to be."

"That has to be true," Billy said. "Why would anybody risk coming out to meet someone and get married otherwise? Especially if they had no means to get back home."

"I don't disagree," Gavin said. "It's just something about her situation doesn't sit right. Like she's hiding something. Maybe it's about her siblings."

"She's got siblings?" Billy opened the package of cookies, then closed it again. Blackened lumps had met their eyes. "Nope. Not even for Meg."

Gavin chuckled, then said, "Yeah. She said she needed the money so that she could adopt her siblings."

"Could be she's worried about them, and that's what you were picking up on," Billy said.

"Maybe." Gavin stood. "I'm heading to the diner for a bite. Join me?"

"I can't," Billy said. "Eli needs to show me the land he's wanting us to buy. Said he showed you the other day when I took the money with Gus for the new cattle?"

"That's right," Gavin agreed. "It's a good spot, but it's going to be difficult to fence it off. That's where your expertise is needed."

"I'll figure out a way." Billy grinned. He waved and left.

Gavin locked the door to the sheriff's office behind him, and headed toward the diner. He wondered what they'd have. Everything was good, but he had his favorites.

He pushed open the door, took his favorite table by the front window, and was surprised to see Miss Anderson walk toward him from the kitchen area.

She seemed startled to see him, and then smiled tentatively. "Hello."

"Hello. Got the job, I see."

"I did," she answered. "It's very busy here, but I am enjoying the work. Are you here for a meal?" When he nodded, she continued, "There's chicken and dumplings today or a beef stew. Which would you rather?"

"Chicken and dumplings," Gavin answered.

"I'll be right back," Miss Anderson said. True to her word, she was back before a minute had passed, a heaping plate before him. She added a basket with two rolls. "Can I get you anything else?"

"Not just yet," Gavin answered.

Miss Anderson nodded and walked over to another table. He watched her as he ate. As always, the meal was good. Madge ran a popular diner, and she and Lisa were fine cooks. He wondered why Madge had never married. She'd make someone a wonderful wife.

Gavin tried not to stare around the diner as he spooned up his meal, but he couldn't help it. Miss Anderson was smiling and bustling around the dining room, fetching drinks and clearing away plates. It was a contrast to the woman who had been in his office a few days ago. Here, she seemed sure of herself. Confident in her duties. Like she didn't have a care in the world, or a secret.

Something about her kept pulling his eyes toward her. It was strange. He wasn't sure what he made of it.

"Enjoy your meal, Sheriff?"

He looked up to see Madge next to the table. "I did. You and Lisa outdid yourselves as usual. Tell her for me."

"I will," Madge answered.

"How's the new woman working out for you?" he asked.

Honestly, he wasn't sure why he asked, other than curiosity.

"She's a hard worker. I'm glad she stopped by. Hannah's a good judge of character. Mirabelle too." Madge patted his arm. "If you want any pie, just let her know."

"I'm stuffed," Gavin said, and motioned to his stomach. "But thank you."

She nodded and walked away, and Gavin stood. Madge was right. Hannah and Mirabelle were good judges of character. So were Eli, Billy, and himself. What was it, then, that kept bugging him? This new role of being sheriff? Had his concerns over being tied down to the job and rules gotten to him? He pulled some money out of his pocket.

"All finished?" Miss Anderson asked as she hurried over.

"Yes. Keep the change for yourself. And, whenever you get off of work, stop by my office. I heard back from the judge," he said, dropping his voice so they wouldn't be overheard.

She took a deep breath and nodded briskly. "I will. I get to leave in an hour for a break. Can I stop by then?"

He nodded and left the diner, stopping to get a newspaper from the post office. As he sat at his desk a few moments later, he realized his mind was wandering. Why? Usually, he didn't have any trouble focusing. Today, however...No. He couldn't even say that. The last few days he'd been having trouble. Ever since the stage came in, and he'd caught that criminal.

But that wasn't it either. He'd caught the man, who had been delivered promptly to the marshals who were hunting him. The reward was nice too, and he put most of it toward the new schoolhouse that was being built.

Gavin sighed and rubbed his eyes. He was tired. That was it. Hadn't been sleeping well. He was still getting used to being alone. It was a little too quiet at times. His state right now had nothing to do with the job, or Miss Anderson.

But if that was the case, why did she pop into his mind just then?

"Sheriff?"

He looked up. Miss Anderson stood just inside the doorway. The sun was bright behind her, almost putting a halo overtop of her. "Come in," he said.

"I hope I wasn't disturbing you," she said a little nervously as she walked closer.

"Not at all." He reached for the note he'd gotten from Judge Jacob Cannon. He'd met him not just because he rode the circuit, but he'd had meals a few times with him at

Eli and Hannah's place. The judge had been her neighbor when she was a child, and she grew up calling him uncle.

"I heard back from the judge," he said, and offered her the note. "I'm afraid there isn't anything you can do." She glanced at it and nodded. "I'm sorry," he continued.

"Don't be. This was all my mistake. I am just grateful the man isn't coming after me for some sort of claim. It's best I simply vanish, truth be told, so my employer doesn't come after me either. Now, I just have to figure out what to do." Her lips were pressed together tightly.

Something tugged at him. "Are you making enough at the diner?" he asked bluntly.

"I make enough for a room. She gives me my meals. There's not much left. But it's not that. I told you. I have younger siblings." She looked down into her lap.

He was quiet. Then, and he didn't know why, he offered, "I can loan you the money to send for them, and the judge can help you with the adoption. I know him well, and I'm sure he will help."

A flash of longing formed on her face, just as quickly replaced by one of defeat. "It's not possible. Thank you, though."

"Why not?" he asked in surprise. "I've got plenty of money. There's no time limit on paying me back."

When she didn't answer, but instead he saw her fingers twitching, Gavin knew he'd hit it. The thing she was hiding. His eyes narrowed as he assessed her. Stiff posture, downturned eyes, worried fidgeting.

"Tell me what you left out the other day," he ordered.

Her head snapped up. "It has nothing to do with the marriage I came here for, so I don't see as it's any of your business."

He hadn't expected that. Her shoulders were squared now, her jaw set, and eyes challenging him.

"It's not," he agreed. He held back the words he wanted to say. Instead, he shrugged. Played it as though he didn't care. Never mind it was eating him up inside.

Miss Anderson studied him now, and Gavin was surprised. Not many people were bold enough to do that. It took everything in him not to fidget or squirm. Was this what his gaze did to others? It was strange to be on the other side of that look.

After a long moment, she seemed to like what she'd seen, for she said, "It's more complicated than simply sending them money for passage or petitioning a judge to adopt them."

"How so? Maybe I can still help." Gavin leaned back in his chair. He was genuine in his offer. If there were kids out there alone, and a few dollars and some help would get them where they needed to go, he wanted to assist. There was no reason he couldn't. Especially as sheriff.

She swallowed hard, and her voice grew quiet. He could hardly hear her and leaned closer. "I don't know where they are. I'd hired someone to keep an eye on them, to keep me updated on their whereabouts. A detective. He'd been updating me for about a year, but I've not heard from him for over two months. I paid him, so I don't think that's the problem. He's just gone...and I don't know where they are or what's happened to them."

That he could help with. Missing persons? He'd done that before many times. A huge part of being a gunslinger was tracking down a bounty.

But before he could say anything, she added, "I just don't know what to do, and I feel that they are in danger. I don't expect you to understand that, but I feel it, and that's why I'm so desperate."

But he did understand it. Good instincts were critical to the job. His job. Always had been.

"And that's why you agreed to the marriage," Gavin told her. "Because you hoped it would give you more means to find them."

"Yes."

"I've tracked down hundreds of people," Gavin said. "It's no problem to track down a few more. I also have a friend—that is all he does. He's good at it. I can get him to go with me. I'll find them, and bring them here to you. Or, you and I can go together. We'll find your siblings easily. Tell me about them, and the last place you know they were." He pulled some paper and a pencil toward himself.

"We can't do that," Miss Anderson said. She was looking at him strangely. "I appreciate your offer, please don't mistake me, but I can't do that. We can't do that."

"Why not? I just told you I could. We could. If it's the money, I won't charge. You live here now, and I help whoever needs me. It's my job."

"It's not that," Miss Anderson said. Her voice rose, nearly sounding panicked. "It's not respectable. We are both unmarried. Sheriff or not, I'm in enough trouble, and I can't let my reputation be compromised. That might prevent me from adopting them, and it also might mean that I'd never get married. I was told most judges would require me to be married in order to adopt."

Was that her problem? It was an easy fix. Gavin shrugged. "So? Marry me. Or pretend to."

The expression on her face made his eyes widen, and Gavin froze. What in the world had he just said?

Chapter 8

Winnie stomped out of the building, heading to the only place where she was sure she could be alone. She'd left the sheriff's office without giving him an answer. The expression of horror she had was likely now etched on her face permanently.

Marry him. Or rather, pretend to marry him. She was in shock. What kind of man was he to think that she'd let her already crumbling chance at a real marriage dissolve further?

To complicate things even more, he was a gunslinger. Though he'd claimed to be a *former* gunslinger, she wasn't quite sure. Did one ever hang up their gunbelt? Not likely, seeing as he was a sheriff. The man must love power. She didn't buy him wanting to help just out of kindness.

Didn't gunslingers always want something in exchange? A favor? Some other sort of recompense?

Had she just gone from one bad situation to another? What would happen now? What if he pressed her? Made demands? Especially those of an inappropriate nature. She was a stranger to this town, and he was in a highly respectable position. In light of her current situation, and the fact she'd been pretending to be Claudette, no one would believe her over him.

Winnie paused in front of the church. The doors were open, and the pews empty. She walked inside. This was what she needed. Silence.

For a long time, she sat. The quiet was a soothing balm to her, but it wasn't enough to loosen the coil of fear that filled her. It had been with her since the day her parents had died of the sickness, and she and her siblings had been thrown into the orphanage.

They'd rarely seen each other. Lillibeth, or Lily as she was nicknamed, was so quiet. So tiny. Her small arms had reached out for Winnie, who'd aged out of the orphanage at sixteen and been sent away. The memory still haunted her. Lily would be seventeen now. Where was she? Was she managing?

And their brother, sixteen, he'd have been pushed out as well. Had he found work? Had he managed to find Lily? Nicholas, or Nick as they called him, had not fared well in the orphanage. Each time she'd been able to snatch a look at him, he'd been sullen, withdrawn, thin.

Tears of anguish burned in Winnie, but she held them in. Tears wouldn't help find her siblings. What had happened to that detective?

Slow and quiet footsteps filled her ears, and Winnie glanced up as Pastor Blackstone sat in the pew with her, though a long space away.

"Good afternoon, Miss Anderson," he said in his calm tone.

"Good afternoon, Pastor," she replied.

"I hope I am not interrupting?" he asked. "If you have come to sit with your thoughts, I can leave, or I can discuss them with you. Whichever you prefer."

How did one answer that? It wasn't like you could just tell a man of God to go away, could you?

Winnie shook her head. "No, I welcome your company." An idea sparked in her mind just then. "And perhaps your advice?"

"Of course." He looked at her with interest. "How might I help?"

"As you know," she started slowly, "I am new to town. I arrived and immediately found myself in a difficult situation. Thanks to a few people, I found myself able to get a job at the diner, and that's helped."

He nodded, but didn't interrupt, so she said, "It was suggested, by the same women who pointed me to the diner, that I ask the sheriff for help with my situation. And that's my problem."

"In what way?" the pastor asked.

"Well, the women seemed very nice. Mrs. Stover at the general store," she watched as he nodded, "and then two women a little older than me perhaps, and I didn't get their last names, but Hannah and Mirabelle. And then I come to find out that these women are married to gunslingers, and the sheriff himself is a former gunslinger."

Winnie realized her voice was trembling, so she stopped and took a deep breath.

"I see. Well, if it sets your mind at ease, I can tell you both of those women are responsible and reputable. Mirabelle is my daughter," he added proudly.

At her surprised look, he smiled. "And, like you, when the gunslingers moved to our town, I had a lot of reservations. They'd done a lot of good, and they still continue to, but I admit, at first I wasn't very sure if I liked them around and if I trusted them."

"What made you change your mind?" Winnie asked. "You must have, seeing as you let your daughter marry one."

He nodded. "I will be very honest with you. I was proud. Too proud. I ended up making a mistake. Because of that, I could have lost Mirabelle. Our town could have been badly vandalized, and I might have also lost the trust that others—including my own wife—placed in me. All because I was more worried about appearances instead of seeing that time and time again, those men have proved themselves to be honest and trustworthy."

"That sounds serious," Winnie said.

"It was," he agreed. "The men, every one of them, are honorable. If they say that they can help, they mean it. Nothing seems to stop them when they have their minds set on something, and in the case of Billy Madison, my daughter's husband, I can tell you there's no better man alive to take care of her and protect her.

"Gavin Jefferson, our sheriff, is his best friend. He's done endless good for our town. Even though he was reluctant to become sheriff, he did it because we needed him. Our town could never pay him what he is worth, or what he used to make in his former profession."

Winnie sat with those thoughts for several minutes, then said, "Thank you, Pastor. That was very helpful. I appreciate knowing that you feel they are good men, and I can trust the sheriff, if I accept his help."

"I promise you, you can," he told her. Another townsperson came in, and he stood, then patted her shoulder. "Come here any time, and I'm always happy to answer any questions you may have."

He slipped away before she could answer, but that suited Winnie just fine. She sat a moment longer, then stood. She'd made up her mind. First, she was going to apologize for storming out. It really had been rude of her. Then, she was going to tell the sheriff that while she appreciated his offer of a pretend marriage to protect her reputation, she couldn't accept it.

If she did, it could lead to trouble getting a husband, and the stability she needed for her siblings. The money, however...that was different. She would not be too proud to accept that, with terms for repayment.

Shoulders back, Winnie went to the sheriff's office and pushed open the door. Her body was trembling and she was terrified, but she blurted out her words anyway. "I'm sorry. I shouldn't have left in anger. You were only trying to help, and I understand that."

To her surprise, he wasn't angry. Concern was what was etched on his face. He walked closer to her, running a hand through his dark hair as he did. "I know it's hard being new in town and unsure who you can trust. I promise, though, you can trust me."

Winnie took a deep breath. "I can't marry you," she said. "It wouldn't be right to pretend such a thing. However, if...if you are willing still to loan me the money, I'll go after them on my own. I'll look for that detective, and if I can't find him, I'll just search on my own. I don't know how soon I'll be able to pay you back, but I will. I'm a woman of my word."

"No." The sheriff shook his head. "That's a bad idea. Even if you find your brother and sister, if they are in danger somehow, how will you get them away? Is it even safe for the three of you to travel alone?"

Winnie opened her mouth and then closed it. They were good points. Not that she'd admit it. So, she wouldn't. "I'll manage," she insisted. "I...always do."

"Why won't you let me help? You don't even have to pay me back. It's a gift." He looked frustrated as he spoke.

She shook her head. "You can't just give someone something like that."

Stubbornly, the sheriff said, "I can if I want."

That was it. She was angry now. How dare he? While the pastor assured her he was a good man, she'd never known anyone—no one at all—who didn't expect something in return. No one gave gifts like that. No one. That was one of the first things she'd learned in the orphanage. There was danger in owing another.

And she planned to tell him so. Her hot temper coursed through her, flaring strongly.

"I might get to live in this town, but you don't get to tell me what to do," Winnie said, nearly nose to nose with the sheriff.

"I'm telling it to you for your own good," he said, his eyes flashing with anger.

"How is it my own good?" she asked, and poked her finger into his chest. She refused to back down. "Do you know what you are? Pushy, that's what. Pushing me to tell you things I didn't want to. Pushing me to accept help

I shouldn't. Pushing me not to repay you. What about what I want? This is my life! Not yours. My siblings. My concern. Mine. I will not let myself be beholden to anyone. So never mind. I won't take anything from you. Not your help, not your dollars."

Her chest was rising and falling heavily, and she was nearly panting. Winnie wasn't sure she'd ever been so angry in her life.

"You don't have to be beholden," he said quietly. "Can't you tell that I want to help? That I'm not here to hurt you? Or trick you or take advantage of you? What is it you want? Tell me." His voice rose. "You frustrate me, woman. Confuse me. Worse, I can't seem to stop thinking about you, wanting to help you, wanting to get to know you better, even though you're little more than a stranger."

Winnie blinked several times. She didn't know what to say at his words. Goosebumps covered her arms, and a chill zipped through her spine. Panic filled her, and an irrational thought came into her mind as she stared into his eyes that pulled her closer and closer.

Winnie didn't let herself stop to think. She was tired of thinking. Tired of doing everything on her own. For one moment, she wanted to do something that was impulsive, even if it was foolish to put her at risk in some way.

This reckless feeling filled every inch of her. Combined with the flames of anger still burning, Winnie didn't care. So, she moved the inch closer, and brought her lips to his.

Chapter 9

The stars were bright, and a hoot owl was calling for a mate. Or to brag about his prey. Gavin wasn't sure. He also wasn't sure what had happened this afternoon. One moment, he and Winnie were nearly shouting at each other, the next, they were locked in a passionate embrace and kiss that ended too soon and with both of them staring in shock at the other.

He wasn't sure who had stepped back first, but they'd each struggled to catch their breath, and the look of her—so wild, so fierce—it had stayed in his mind and refused to budge.

If it hadn't been for the town bell ringing the hour, and her gasp she had to get back to work, Gavin thought he might have pulled her in for another kiss. Or asked her what she'd been thinking.

He couldn't, though. He was sheriff. Respectable. Had to look out for others and not think about what he wanted. Play by the rules of society. Of the law.

But what about him? And what did he want?

That was something he still didn't know yet. The memory of her lips on his, the fire burning in her, and then that look of surprise. Not fear, not embarrassment, but surprise. It made him wonder even more about her. Made him wonder if she might be the kind of woman willing to accept both a former gunslinger and a sheriff as her man.

He liked her. There was no doubt in his mind. Even before she'd kissed him, he was feeling that way. But she'd refused his help. His money. Why? He had both he could offer. So, what was it about the situation she didn't like?

Gavin tensed. Maybe it wasn't the situation. Maybe it was him. He strode from the porch to inside the house and over to the small mirror in his room. He studied himself carefully. His hair was a little long, his skin a little worn from the sun. Gavin glanced down at his hands. They were calloused from hard work. His boots caught his eye next. Well worn, they were comfortable, though they'd seen better days.

That must be it. She didn't want to pretend she was married to him, because she thought that he was too rough.

Well, he could fix that. After all, he'd won the eye of many women. He already knew how to be polite. He just had to change his appearance a little. Cut his hair short. Look more respectable. Lose his old and favorite boots. Show her he was a man who—

"It's a bad idea."

Gavin turned, gun in his hand. It was only the fact that the words registered a split second later it was Eli's voice that made him release his finger that was on the trigger and about to squeeze.

"Don't you knock?" Gavin growled.

"I did," Eli said, a smirk on his face. "Never thought I'd see the day, you not hearing someone ride up, walk up the porch, knock, and open the door."

Gavin stuffed his gun back at his waist. "I've got a lot on my mind," he muttered.

"That so? She about five foot four, new to town, and working at the diner?"

The smirk in Eli's voice was enough to make Gavin's anger flare if it had been anyone other than him or Billy talking, but he couldn't be angry at one of his oldest friends.

Instead, he asked, "Hannah ever want you to change?"

"Change? What do you mean?" Eli asked as he walked into the kitchen.

Gavin followed and sat at the table while Eli poured two mugs of freshly pressed apple cider. "I mean," he said, taking one of the mugs and toying with it, "Hannah ever want you to be different? Your hair or your clothes? Your manners?"

"Nope." Eli shook his head. "It's a bad idea to be involved with someone who wants that. You already know that. This woman tell you to change something?"

"No." Gavin was quiet a moment. "Her name's Winifred Anderson. She didn't, but...well, I can't think what else it is."

"What else what is?" Eli asked quietly.

Gavin looked into his friend's eyes. They were understanding. Non judging. There was no humor, only concern. It was hard to look into them, so he dropped his gaze to his mug.

After a deep breath, he said, "I offered her help. Hannah probably told you, she's new to town and thought she'd be here getting married, but that didn't work out. Turns out she's worried about her younger siblings. She hired a detective to keep her updated on them while she was a maid, and while she tried to find a man to marry so she could adopt them."

"I'm guessing something's happened on that end, since she also didn't get wed," Eli said.

"Correct. She's also not heard from the detective for a while, and feels it in her gut something's wrong," Gavin sighed, then drank deeply from his mug.

"Then it likely is," Eli said. "And you offered help."

"I did." Gavin lowered his mug. "But she didn't want it. Said it wasn't respectable for her to travel with me, us being unmarried. So, I told her we could pretend to be married."

Eli barked out laughter. "Oh, I bet that went well."

"It...didn't," Gavin agreed. "I don't understand what's happened. I offered to pay for the kids, offered to take her with me. I'm going to call in Ryan Lundy to help me track down the kids."

"He's the best," Eli said, then added, "when one of us or Nathan Wick isn't around."

Gavin nodded. "Well, anyway, she got all upset at me. Talked a whole bunch of nonsense. Made it seem like I was trying to bank a favor. I wasn't."

With a slow nod, Eli said, "I've seen that before. Usually from people who've had a difficult time."

"I know," Gavin sighed. "But I wasn't going to do that. I don't even need her to pay me back."

"So all this has something to do with you staring in the mirror, distracted like?" Eli asked.

"I just was wondering if I cut my hair, maybe got new clothes... As sheriff, I guess I need to conform more. Be more..." Gavin didn't finish his thought.

"No." Eli reached over and smacked him on the shoulder. "The town chose you for who you were. If they'd wanted someone else, they'd have asked for them. You don't need to be different to be sheriff." He crossed his arms. "And didn't you say yourself if you have to change for someone because of what they expect, that isn't love?"

"Who's saying anything about love?" Gavin asked.

"You didn't have to." Eli grinned. "I can smell it a mile away. Now, tell me what you know, and I'll share any ideas I have."

* * *

When Eli left an hour later, Gavin felt a little lighter. And a little guilty. He'd managed to keep the kiss he'd had with Miss Anderson private, but now, as soon as he was alone with his thoughts again, she—and her lips pressed to his—were right back in his mind.

Eli was right, though; he knew that. When the job of sheriff had come up, he hadn't wanted to take it. Hadn't wanted to change who he was. And he didn't. No one had said a thing about it. So, why would he consider doing that now? Being who he wasn't? No. If Miss Anderson liked him or not, that was her business. Not his. His job was to help those in need in this town, and that's what he was going to do.

Gavin got some paper and scratched out a note to Ryan Lundy. He hadn't seen him for about two years, maybe three. They'd worked together several times in the past, though. If Ryan couldn't help him, he'd send word to Nathan Wick. Though he'd hung up his gunbelt and was a married man now, Gavin was sure he and Eli would assist him in looking for these two missing kids if he asked.

He put the letter in an envelope, and set it near the front door so he wouldn't forget it in the morning. It was getting late and he was tired, but not so tired he thought he'd be able to sleep.

It was a proven fact, when three hours later, he was still awake. Every time his eyes closed, even just a blink's worth, an image of Miss Anderson, eyes blazing and lips on his, came to mind.

He had it bad. And he didn't know what to do.

Chapter 10

Four days had passed since she'd embarrassingly grabbed the sheriff and kissed him. Winnie still didn't know why she had. She'd been so angry one moment, and the next...completely taken in by the fact she realized he was genuine in wanting to help her.

As far back as she thought, Winnie couldn't ever remember someone wanting to help her just to help her, no strings attached. But it was more than that. She'd seen him around town, and she'd been watching him ever since they'd first met to see if his façade would slip. It hadn't. Which meant he really was as good as everyone said.

She wouldn't lie to herself and try to hide the fact she also found him attractive. Was there a chance he thought the same? Not so that she could have a pretend marriage, but to know, after her bruised ego with Mr. Duncan, that someone would find her attractive. Perhaps even want a relationship with her.

There was no time for that, though, not until her sister and brother were safe and with her. Winnie fretted about them constantly. That is, when her mind wasn't filled with thoughts of the sheriff. Where were they? Where was that detective? Something had happened, that's all there was to it.

"You've done a great job," Madge said as she wiped her hand across her forehead. "You are worth both the girls I had earlier."

Winnie flushed with pleasure at the kind words. "I enjoy it here," she said. "And I appreciate the job."

"I appreciate our two-hour break," Lisa said. "My feet are killing me."

Madge nodded as she nearly collapsed in one of the kitchen chairs. "Yes. It's beautiful outside. I'd go get some fresh air if I weren't so tired. What an incredible lunch rush we had."

"It's that new pie of yours," Winnie said. "Everyone loves it."

"It's a wonder what a little recipe tinkering can do." Lisa nodded. She glanced at Winnie. "You going out for a little fresh air?"

"I am," Winnie said. "It's too beautiful for me to stay in. I'll be back in plenty of time."

Madge simply waved her hand lazily. "Enjoy yourself."

Winnie slipped out the kitchen door and breathed in deeply. It was the perfect day. Blue skies, a fresh breeze, neither too warm nor too cold. Perfection.

She slowly strolled past the shops, letting her eyes soak in everything. With her pay, she'd been frugal, getting only the absolute necessities. Every cent must go toward her siblings.

The sheriff's office rose in front of her and she hesitated. Should she cross the street so he didn't see her? Winnie bit her lip and had just about planned to do so, when the office door opened and someone ran right into her.

"Sorry," the figure said. A moment later, she recognized the sheriff.

"It was my fault," she answered, and tried to hurry away. She couldn't bear to look at him. What would he think about her and the fact she'd nearly attacked him so wantonly the last time they'd spoken?

"Wait, I was on my way to find you," he told her. "Have a moment to talk?"

Winnie stiffened. She opened her mouth to decline when he said, "It's about your sister and brother."

That made her look up. She hesitated, then nodded. "Of course."

He reopened the office door and allowed her to go in first. She shivered as she walked in and past *the spot*. The spot where they'd stood so close and then...

Winnie sucked in a breath. Perhaps what was worst of all, was she had no remorse over the fact.

"You can sit if you like," he said, and she startled. She hadn't realized she was so lost in her thoughts he was already in his chair at his desk.

Winnie shook her head and folded her hands. "What is it you wanted to see me about?" she asked, still standing.

"I wrote a friend of mine. He's a tracker. One of the best. If there's a chance of finding someone, he will. He's ready to leave and look for them the moment he knows more."

She tensed. While she wasn't sure why he'd done that, she also wasn't sure how to answer. A man like that must be very expensive, and she'd never have the funds for him.

As if he knew what she was thinking, he added, "He's not charging. He's doing it because we're friends. I've helped him before, and he's helped me. We don't keep score. We're just there for each other."

She couldn't imagine such a thing. Why was he telling her that? Was he trying to reassure her about the cost? Or shame her because she'd refused his help earlier?

"If we're going to help your siblings, you have to tell me everything. You can't hold anything back. I know what you've told me, but I think there's something missing." The sheriff crossed his arms over his chest. "Trust me," he said, softening his voice. "I promise I won't let you down."

The words shocked her very being. Winnie closed her eyes, and then slowly blinked them open. She'd heard those words so many times. *Trust me. I promise I won't let you down.* But never had she believed them until now.

But the fact that he was willing to do that scared her far more than she wanted to admit. It was for the simple reason of what if. What if she did trust him? Did believe him? What if he could help her, what then?

The fact of the matter was the sheriff had been haunting her thoughts and her dreams. That kiss had been a catalyst. More than that, it had been a glimpse of something that she wanted and she could never have.

Aware she'd been silent for too long, Winnie met his eyes. "I can't," she said softly.

"Is it because you don't trust me?" he asked, getting up and coming closer. He perched on the edge of his desk.

She was quiet, and looked at her boots. How could she answer that? She didn't—couldn't—trust anyone. Each time she'd tried, she had been let down. Hurt. Betrayed. She just couldn't do it anymore.

Winnie took a deep breath. "It's because they are my responsibility. They were mine to take care of, and I failed. So they are mine to protect and rescue or whatever else I need to do."

That included doing it on her own, so she didn't owe anyone anything she couldn't repay. No matter what he said, there was sure to be a cost.

A gentle touch on her cheek made Winnie raise her head. The sheriff was looking at her with compassion. It would be her undoing. She was sure of it.

"There's nothing wrong with asking for help," he said gently, "or accepting it. It doesn't make you less of anything."

"But I can't repay you," she said, closing her eyes and praying the tears didn't squeeze through her lashes.

"I don't need a repayment," he said. His words were filled with truth. "I've more money than I could spend in a lifetime."

"Everyone wants repayment of some kind," she said, her voice trembling. "And most of those things, I can't and I won't do."

His hand dropped from her cheek to her shoulder and slid down her arm. The trail of his touch felt like a fire licking at her sleeve. She was shocked it hadn't burned away.

"Not everyone wants something," he said.

"I've never known someone who doesn't," Winnie said, her eyes locked on his fingers.

"Fine," the sheriff said. "I do want something."

Winnie tensed and looked at his face. She knew it. But he kept talking before she could say anything.

"I want to see you happy. I want to see you smile. I want to..." He stopped then, and his eyes searched her face. "I want to know you better," he finished.

That wasn't what she'd expected. The air was filled with a crackling energy. Winnie met his eyes and felt herself lost in them. What would happen if she kissed him again? They were so close. The sheriff was holding one of her hands. When had that happened? Winnie shivered. She wanted to step closer. Let him help her, let him protect her and her siblings.

But her fear wouldn't let her. Winnie stepped back, and gently pulled her hand free. She took another step toward the door.

"You can't keep doing that," the sheriff said. "Leaving."

She turned and gave him a sad look. She wanted to believe him. But time and time again, she'd learned you couldn't trust anyone. "I can do whatever I think I have to."

And then, she closed the door behind her and sagged against it, her eyes filling with hot tears.

Chapter 11

She'd left him. Again. And this time she'd nearly run out. What did that mean? That he was so disgusting, so unsuitable for a woman like her, she couldn't even bear to look at him?

Was the problem that he was pushing too much, like she'd said? Perhaps he'd made her mission his own, without her acceptance.

Maybe he'd scared her off when he confessed how she was making him feel, and what he wanted. It was all true, though, every word. Maybe he shouldn't have said it. He forgot for a time that he was the sheriff. Had only thought about the fact he was a man, set on helping the woman who needed him. Who he was sure he could help and make happy and love.

Gavin paced around the sheriff's office. He wished his violin was nearby. It would soothe him. Distract him. He just wanted to help. That was all. Why wouldn't she let him?

Then, a terrible thought came to his mind. It near punched him in the gut. Her siblings. What if she was lying about them? It wouldn't have been her first lie. She'd pretended to be someone else for the chance of a wedding to a well-off man. What if she was trying to get some sort of sympathy? Made up the siblings?

Except that didn't make sense, and his instincts told him that wasn't it. Besides, her story would be too easy to check out. He knew her name, could search for her past if he really wanted to.

No, the truth was more likely that she didn't like something about him. His thoughts turned back to that night he'd considered changing himself. It wasn't too late if he wanted to.

But, it was obvious, even if he had an attraction to Miss Anderson, she didn't have one for him. They weren't even on a first-name basis. She was keeping a distance between them. Gavin never thought it could have hurt as much as it did. Sure, he'd been sympathetic with Billy's heartache and frustration over feeling helpless with Mirabelle, but this was something completely different. A whole new level.

He didn't like it.

Gavin sat himself down to tackle the notices that had come from other towns. There was a new wanted poster. He studied the image of the man for a moment, then set it aside. He'd hang it out shortly.

The office door opened, and he glanced up to see Hannah walking toward him with a basket. He couldn't help it. He cringed.

Hannah caught the motion and laughed. "It's not Meg's cookies," she promised.

Gavin laughed too. "I'm sorry. Don't tell her I did that."

"I won't," she said cheerfully. "Anyway, she's on to biscuits now."

"Oh. How are those going?" he asked.

The look on her face told him all he needed to know. Taking after her mother in the kitchen, she was not, but there was plenty of time. Hannah was a wonderful mother, and as patient and caring as anyone could ever be.

"I did bring you a bite, though," she said. "I knew I'd be passing through, and we had so much left from an early dinner I wanted to bring you some."

"That was kind of you," he said. "I appreciate it."

Hannah set the basket on his desk, and he looked inside. "Fried chicken. That's my favorite. Eli is a lucky man," he said, reaching for a piece.

"We're all lucky that you and Billy stayed in town," she said. "And that you sacrificed to become sheriff."

Gavin set down the chicken he'd picked up. "Hannah, can I ask you a question?"

At her nod, he asked, almost hesitating, "You're a woman. And you're almost like my sister, so I can trust you to be truthful, and also discreet?"

"Of course," Hannah answered. Her eyes filled with worry. "What's wrong?"

"I don't know. I keep wondering that myself. Never in my life have I ever had to work at getting a woman to smile at me. They just flocked to me. Not as often as they did Billy, but I had my share of attention."

She looked at him sympathetically. "And someone you've got your eye on isn't noticing?"

"Something like that," he said. "I thought about maybe if I changed how I looked?"

"Don't do it," she said, crossing her arms. "Any woman worth anything wouldn't want that. You wouldn't be you anymore, either."

He didn't answer.

She squeezed his hand. "You are a special person, Gavin. I think this woman, whoever she is, likely knows that. She just might be scared."

"Scared? Of what?" he asked. Her words were confusing. "She's got a lot of fire in her."

"That doesn't mean she isn't intimidated by you," Hannah said. "She also might have a lot on her mind. Things that are distracting her. When Eli first came, I had so much going on, that even though I knew I was falling in love with him, I was scared to show it. Scared to let myself get hurt again. Drawn in past the point of no return. Maybe it's the same for this woman.

"You've always had confidence, as long as I've known you," she continued. "Don't let this confuse you. Don't doubt who you are."

He was quiet a moment, then said, "You're all right. I'm glad Eli picked you."

Her cheeks pinked. "Me too." She leaned in close and whispered, "We might be adding to our family soon."

Gavin couldn't stop the grin on his face. He hugged Hannah, glad Eli had answered her ad all those months ago and asked him and Billy to help out. Once she'd left, he ate the meal she'd brought. He felt fortunate to be here in Red Ridge. Eli and Billy had always been family, but now he had Hannah, Gus, and Mirabelle. Once he got used to the house being so lonely, he was sure he'd enjoy it more.

Family wasn't something he'd had much of growing up. He couldn't remember his folks. An aunt and uncle raised him and as soon as they could, told him to make his own way. He'd fallen into gunslinging as it was the fastest way to make both money and a reputation. More often than not, it was the reputation that kept a man alive. He'd earned it, though, and worked hard for it.

Gavin picked up the wanted poster, a hammer, and some tacks. A thought came to him just then. Yeah. He'd always worked hard for what he wanted. To be a fast and accurate shot. To be smart and a good tracker. So this…whenever he was ready for it, a family of his own and a chance at love?

Maybe he had to work for that too. And he'd always gotten where he needed to by being himself. He wouldn't change that. Not for anyone, not for anything.

Determination filled him now. He'd let himself stew for too long. Worry needlessly. That was done. Things would either work out or they wouldn't.

He stepped outside and started to put the sign in place. He'd just gotten the last tack hammered in when a bloodcurdling scream filled his ears.

Chapter 12

It was nice to escape the diner. The dinner rush had been exhausting, but at the tail end, Madge had asked her to carry meals to the men who worked at the livery and then told her that was her last task for the day, and she could go back to her boarding house.

The short walk with a stiff breeze had restored her energy somewhat, and now that her basket had been delivered and her hands were free, she held them out to feel the wind rush between her fingers.

It was a little childlike, she knew, but the wind here in Oregon was incredible. She'd thought only the plains had great winds, but here, at times the mountains blocked things, and at others sent it whistling down. It was a curious phenomenon that she couldn't wait to share with her siblings.

Her siblings. Winnie's mood instantly darkened. Lily and Nick. What were they doing right now? She hoped they were happy, with full bellies and sturdy clothes on their backs, and a few dollars in their possession. And together. If they were together, then they'd be okay. Soon she'd find them, somehow. Once she did, they'd be together again, and she'd be able to see they were taken care of.

Even more importantly, she'd be doing it without owing anyone any favors. That meant nothing could separate them again.

Winnie turned the corner of the stable. She was near the attached corral, where several horses were grazing. She stopped to admire them. A sudden gust of wind hit her, and she felt her hat shift. Just as she reached for it, it blew away. Frantically, her fingers scrambled after it, but the wind deposited it just out of reach. About twelve feet away in the corral.

"Oh no! That's my only hat," Winnie groaned. She glanced about. No one was around, and the horses weren't paying attention. Maybe she could slip in and get it. She hated to disturb the men she'd just delivered dinner to.

A large black horse—she had no idea what kind—was between her and her hat. "I'll just slip around him," Winnie said confidently. "I must have my hat."

Glancing around once more to be sure no one would see her unladylike display of ankle, Winnie hoisted her foot onto the lower rail of the fence, then grabbed on to the top and pulled herself astride. She jumped down, narrowly avoided a deposit of horse manure, and straightened her skirt.

"There. That wasn't so bad," she panted, a little out of breath from her exertion. She fixed her eye on her hat and strode toward it.

But she hadn't expected that her being unfamiliar to the horse, and the wind, which swirled her skirt around frantically, would spook the horse.

Winnie froze for a moment, as the horse stamped its feet, and started to crow hop, letting out a whinny that made Winnie's blood run cold and her pulse race.

The large black animal let out another frightening sound while trying to get away from her hat, which had been picked up by another gust of wind, and slid toward it. The horse bucked and spun, making Winnie rush back toward the fence with a scream.

However, her movements further spooked the horse, and it moved toward her, pressing her against the fence. Hooves were raised, the head tossed side to side, and the horse's eyes were wide with fear.

"Help!" Winnie screamed, as she tried to climb. She was pinned and scared. "Help me!"

The horse was angry, and belatedly, Winnie realized her screams startled it more. It was stamping, making angry sounds, and Winnie was sure this was it. She'd be killed, all for her silly hat.

"Whoa there," a voice said, calm and right next to her.

Winnie cracked her eyes open. She'd squeezed them closed, not wanting to see her impending doom. She was surprised to see she wasn't alone.

The sheriff was there, one hand on the horse, another holding a rope.

"I've got him," one of the men from the livery said, coming into the corral with her and the sheriff.

The sheriff continued to speak calmly, in a soothing tone. He let one hand run along the sleek dark neck of the horse. Winnie dared to glance at the beast. It was calming down. She just wished she could say the same about herself.

The livery man approached the horse, gave some sort of strange whistle, and the horse, suddenly docile, trotted right toward him.

Just as Winnie felt certain her legs were going to collapse from fear, two arms wrapped around her and lifted her up.

"Are you hurt?"

She looked up into the sheriff's face. "M-m-my hat. It-it blew away," she stammered, trying to explain.

"Got it right here, miss," one of the other livery men said. He shook his head. "Next time, get one of us. He's aggressive, this horse. He's a green-broke stallion who spooks right easily. You were in more danger than you know."

Had she not been held, Winnie knew she'd have fainted. All of that, because of her hat. She clutched it with one hand, and her other wrapped around the sheriff's neck as he carried her out a gate.

Once outside the corral, he looked deeply into her eyes. "Should I set you down?"

Winnie ought to say yes. She wasn't acting like herself. Usually, she was confident, self assured. But her heart was also still pounding, the sheriff's arms were strong, and she didn't want to embarrass herself further if she were to be wobbly.

Yet, she was in public, in his arms, and that didn't bode well for her reputation or chance at finding a husband.

"Yes, please," she whispered, hoping that her legs would hold.

Slowly and gently, he set her on her feet, but kept an arm around her for support. Once Winnie felt as though she were able to stand, she nodded briskly at him, and he pulled his arm away.

"Thank you," Winnie said. Her cheeks were crimson. "I feel like such a fool."

"It was a chance for me to play hero." He grinned, giving her a wink.

She liked his smile, and it brought one to her face, as well as a small laugh. "I...I ought to go," she said. Then she stopped. "But I don't want to. Could I stay with you for a little, please, until I calm down?"

"Of course. Are you up for a walk? There's a small garden near the church and some benches. It's a quiet place, private too. Not," he added, "that I'm trying to take advantage of you."

"I understand," Winnie said. She nodded. "That sounds nice."

They walked slowly away from the livery, and along an alleyway. Winnie appreciated the fact the sheriff was leading her a different, more secluded way to the church. She wasn't looking forward to walking past anyone who might look at her strangely, if they'd seen what had happened.

He led her to the church, then behind it she saw the garden he'd told her about. Rose bushes dotted the area, and there was a small walking path that led to several benches. Winnie took one, then breathed in the rose-scented air. How had she not discovered this place sooner? She closed her eyes, and tried to relax.

They sat in silence, the sheriff next to her. She replayed the last few moments over and over, and didn't realize it until he reached to put an arm around her that she was shaking.

"I'm sorry," Winnie said. "I think I only just realized how badly things could have turned out."

He nodded, removed his arm, and said, "I won't lie. I was feeling concerned. I'm glad you aren't hurt."

"Me too. Your timing was serendipitous."

"Miss Anderson—"

"Winnie," she interrupted. "I think after that incident, we are familiar enough to be on a first-name basis."

He chuckled. "Winnie, then. I'm Gavin, in case you've forgotten."

She hadn't. In fact, she'd whispered his name to herself several times after their kiss, just to see how it sounded.

Winnie took in a deep breath. "I need to apologize."

"For climbing in the corral?" he asked.

"No. For…withholding some of the details about my past. You'd asked me to tell them all. In truth, none are pertinent to finding my siblings. I was honest in that. I didn't want to tell you everything because I was embarrassed."

"You've nothing to be embarrassed about," he assured her.

Winnie focused on a rose a short distance away. Its peach-colored petals were tinged with red. What would it smell like?

After a moment, her eyes still on the flower, she spoke. "I admit that I have had to do so much on my own for so long, I have a hard time accepting help. Even from someone who insists there's no repayment needed."

"Is that why you lied to me?" he asked.

"I told you. I didn't lie." She looked at him in confusion.

"You also didn't tell the truth. The whole truth. I don't think you realize how every detail is important. And how it might mean the difference between rescuing your siblings or something happening to them." He fixed his eyes on hers, seriously. "What might seem unimportant to you, might be the key to helping them."

"I see. I didn't realize that. I still don't understand it, but fine. I'll tell you everything." Winnie took a deep breath. "I just hope you don't judge me harshly."

Chapter 13

When Gavin had come across Miss Anderson—Winnie, as she now asked him to call her—with the large and spooked horse pressing against her, his heart had nearly stopped. It had only been instinct that had spurred him into action. She'd been so small up against the large stallion. It was a wonder she hadn't been kicked by him.

Another moment and she might not still be breathing.

But he wouldn't think about that. Her innocence in not understanding you didn't just get into a pen with an animal you didn't know caused him to shake his head. City folk. Just like they didn't understand you didn't go meandering on someone's property, even if there's no house nearby, you didn't go toward a strange animal. Especially one bigger than you. Any animal, if it felt spooked or threatened, could lash out, sometimes in a most devastating way.

Luckily, her scream had alerted the men in the livery, and they also had sprung into action.

Gavin was sure, though, that just like he wouldn't be able to erase her terrified expression from his memory, he also wouldn't be able to forget the feel of her in his arms, even though it was only for a moment. She fit perfectly. Her lips had trembled, and it was all he could do to hold himself back from capturing them once more.

As she sat now, distress upon her lovely face, Gavin hoped that whatever she told him wouldn't be as bad as she seemed to think it was.

"Several years ago, a sickness spread through our town," she began. "I think a quarter of the town was lost. My parents were among them. We had no nearby family, but there was an aunt about a day's travel. When we arrived at her home, she kept us for a few weeks, decided it was too much work to have three extra mouths to feed, and sent us to an orphanage."

Her eyes were focused on something in the garden, unwilling to meet his. "Lily and I were able to stay together, as we were girls. It wasn't often I saw Nick. When I was sixteen, I was made to leave. I promised my sister and brother that when they were released, I would be nearby and find them and we'd be a family again."

"Is that when you lost track of them?" Gavin asked.

"Yes. Lily is seventeen now, and Nick sixteen. But I've heard nothing at all. I'd sent my address to the orphanage once I started my job. When Lily was sixteen and a month had passed without hearing from her, I wrote the orphanage asking her whereabouts, and seeking information about Nick as well. I was told neither of them were there and had not been for some time."

"Did they run away?" Gavin asked.

"I don't think so. After I hired the detective, he discovered that quite a few older children were missing from the orphanage. Of course, being orphans, it's not really talked about or a concern when one goes missing. They have no family, so who would notice?" Her tone was filled with sadness.

"I didn't have an easy time when I left. It was just by chance that I was chosen as a companion for an older woman. The opportunity was a blessing. I was able to learn manners and proper ways of speech and dress. It's served me well over the years because people thought I was of a higher class, as I was a traveling companion, not just a servant. That is what helped me get my most recent position, the one that...led me here.

"The woman who took me in at first taught me something important. No one wants to help someone who's poor and uneducated, and I knew it would be impossible to provide for my siblings without either an income or a successful marriage, so I worked hard to educate myself, so I'd have the opportunity to help Lily and Nick."

"It's never a bad thing to be educated," he agreed.

"Perhaps, though, that's why I ended up in this mess. I let the position of my new job, the money I was making, and the idea that I could take care of things on my own go to my head. Then, I let myself get talked into pretending I was of a higher class than I genuinely am in order to marry a man who could give me just what I wanted. Opportunity."

"Some people and their classes," Gavin said, shaking his head. "In my opinion, there's only people. They do good things, they do bad things. But at the end of the day, we're all people. All put our shoes on one at a time. Even those fancy ladies you worked for."

She laughed quietly. "I suppose you are right."

Gavin studied her for a moment. "You know, I thought you were looking down on me."

"Why would you think that?" Winnie asked, her eyes wide.

He shrugged. "Small town western sheriff. Gunslinger. Those two things don't usually go together, and not everyone thinks highly of someone out this way. Matter of fact, I thought about changing myself. Proving that I was good enough."

"Good enough for what?" she questioned.

"For you." Gavin let his words hang in the air as he thought about just what he'd contemplated. Cutting his hair, hanging up his guns. Becoming the kind of man a woman like her would want. Rich. Safe. Boring.

As she looked at him, he continued, "But the more I thought about it, I didn't like the idea of not being true to myself. Not doing the things I'm good at. The things that help others. My friends reminded me I didn't need a change. I do a good job at being myself. I didn't need to pretend to be someone or something I wasn't, just to set someone else at ease. Maybe your boss was right on some things, but she wasn't right on all of them."

"There is truth in what you say, and I apologize if I made you feel that way. I wouldn't change anything about you," Winnie told him. She shook her head. "You are perfect just as you are. I don't know how you could think otherwise.

"I think…my years in the orphanage filled me with distrust of others. No favors were given without something expected in return, often something you wouldn't be willing to do. So, when you offered your help, I reverted to that mindset. I see how wrong I was. You've been nothing but kind, and I am ashamed of how I suspected you of anything untoward."

"But?" Gavin asked, sensing the unspoken word.

"But it has been my experience that no one will like me if I'm myself. More importantly, no one will love me. I…I have nothing to offer."

Her eyes met his as she spoke, and Gavin wanted nothing more than to tell her how wrong she was. How very, very wrong. It was obvious Winnie didn't notice the stares of the men in town. He was sure at least a dozen of them had fallen in love with her.

Why was it she felt she had nothing to offer? That no one would like her true self? Gavin felt fortunate that even though he'd had moments of discontent with her, that he felt like he was getting to know her. The real her.

Fiery. Determined. Selfless.

So, to hear her say such a thing, it nearly cracked his heart.

Winnie took in a shuddering breath. She tried to smile, but it was forced.

Gavin stared at her for a moment. She thought no one could love her. There was nothing further from the truth. An electric feeling filled the air as she waited for his reply, and then, as the words sprang from his lips without warning, he answered her, "I will."

Chapter 14

Winnie's breath caught in her chest. What had he meant when he said, "I will"? Did that mean he'd like her? Love her? It couldn't be that, could it? Her mind raced over the words, trying to connect them to what she'd said.

The feelings she'd had for him, ones that seemed to grow despite her trying to smother them, threatened to burst to the surface.

Her eyes widened, and she shook her head. "I...don't know what you mean."

"Then I'll tell you." Gavin moved closer.

It wasn't much, just a few inches, but it suddenly felt like he was too close. There was nowhere for her to go though, unless she stood, so Winnie tried to act as though she were calm, and not feeling dizzy from her heart that was beating far too quickly from his nearness.

"I've never been interested in settling down, but after we met, something changed. A feeling that I just wanted to get closer, even though I didn't know why. It near ate me up inside, especially when you refused my help. I knew—knew surer than anything I've ever felt—that there was something special about you. You don't give yourself enough credit. You think no one would like you? Love you if you are yourself?"

Gavin gestured widely. "There's an entire world out there filled with people who would. Likely already do, far more than you know. People who want to be your friend. Those who want to give you love. Have your love. People..." he dropped his voice, "like me. I see you. Understand how you feel. I know who you are, and it doesn't make me want to run away. It makes me want to come closer. If you'll let me."

Winnie shivered as goosebumps broke out over her skin. She knew he was right. He did understand her. But how? The words he said struck a chord in her, and Winnie realized just how much she'd needed to hear them. To feel accepted for who she was. Winifred Anderson. The girl from the orphanage. The young woman who had made a life for herself. The woman who found herself falling in love with a gunslinger.

"You don't need to answer me. You don't even have to return my affection. Just know that you are an incredible person. You are strong, you are hardworking, you are relentless in your pursuit to get what you want. I see those things, because they are echoes of myself." He looked at her, almost sadly. "But you cannot think that no one would care for you, as your true self. It's not true, and you deserve to know that."

"Who are you?" she whispered.

Her words meant so much more, but it was as though he understood the question. Gavin reached up and brushed her hair from off her cheek.

"I'm someone who doesn't play by the rules. Someone who goes in guns out and figures out the consequences later. Someone who understands what it's like not to have a family."

Her breath caught at that. Was it true? Was that part of the connection that she felt with him?

Her eyes searched his. He was telling the truth. Somehow, she knew he'd accept her, no matter what. And if she wanted more with him, he'd give it. Winnie wanted that. At least, she thought she did. Right now, however, her thoughts were too focused on Lily and Nick. She had to find them. Had to help them if they needed her. It wasn't until that happened that she'd be able to relax enough to figure out what it was she wanted.

But he seemed to know that too.

The door burst open. Gavin dropped his hands from her face. She felt suddenly empty. A boy, perhaps twelve, rushed in.

"For you, Sheriff," he said.

"Thanks," Gavin answered, taking the offered letter and handing over a coin.

The boy rushed out just as quickly as he'd come. Winnie followed Gavin's movements as he tore open the envelope. His body tensed as he read whatever was written down.

"What is it?" she whispered, sensing something terrible.

Gavin's eyes sought hers. In them, storms swirled. He offered the letter to her. "It's about your brother and sister."

It was all Winnie could do not to snatch the paper from him. "You've found them?"

"Not me. But, yes."

Her eyes scanned the note. It was short and to the point. Her heart squeezed painfully at the words, while her stomach churned.

Gavin, I found them both, but it's not good. You better get here quick if you want a chance to rescue them before things get worse. The detective she'd hired has been killed, and the kids were sold to a criminal organization. I've tracked them to a saloon where the girl will start working while the boy gets trained to be one of their operatives. –Ryan

"I knew it," Winnie whispered, feeling the strength leave her legs. She reached for the wall to steady herself. "I knew something was wrong. I just didn't expect it to be this bad." She stared at the paper. What would she do? How could she help?

Fear filled every inch of her. "What if we are too late? This is all my fault. I wasted time. Why didn't I seek them sooner when I'd not heard from the detective? It's possible I made their situation worse. There must have been something more I could have done."

"There wasn't," Gavin told her. His lips kept moving, but she couldn't hear whatever he was saying overtop the absolute terror she was feeling.

Winnie's thoughts began to swirl around and around, faster than she could grab on to them. The letters on the message blurred as she stared at them, almost willing them not to be true.

How had this happened? How were they sold? Someone was responsible. She might never learn who, but she wouldn't stop doing whatever she had to in order to rescue them.

Her sister...to be used to *entertain.* Her brother, to be introduced to a life of crime. A horrible guilt filled Winnie. She hadn't done enough for them. There were amends to be made, but those would come later.

Right now, she had to get there. Right away.

"Hey." Gavin drew her attention.

"What?" she asked. She frowned. Couldn't he see she was thinking?

He winked at her. "I'm going after your siblings. Are you coming with me?"

Chapter 15

"You can't go." Winnie's voice was flat, and it startled Gavin. It wasn't what he'd expected to hear. What he thought might happen would be she'd shed some tears of joy. Women did that, didn't they? Maybe ones of hope. A gasp, her hands to her mouth. Some gratitude. The woman sure didn't seem to know how to say thank you.

How many times had he offered help and she'd refused? Or gotten angry. He'd lost count by now. So, not even surprised by her reaction since he'd had time to think it through, he raised a brow. "Oh?"

"I won't risk you getting killed. I'll never be able to get over the guilt I feel at the detective being murdered. I can't live with knowing I might do the same to you."

"We don't know he was murdered. It could have been an illness. An accident," Gavin said, though he did, for a fact, know it was true. He'd gotten a note from another lawman, and the name and the cause of death matched that of the detective. There was no need to upset her more by telling her this now. The kids' rescue—and Winnie—needed to be his focus.

"I will take care of this myself," Winnie replied stiffly. "I'm very good at thinking up solutions for problems."

"You don't have a lot of time," Gavin warned. "And there's already a good solution." He pointed to himself.

"No."

Gavin shook his head. She was stubborn. But it didn't matter. He was going after the kids and leaving tomorrow. If he had to lock her up in his jail he would, if that's what it took to keep her safe. She didn't know how to get them back. He did. Therefore, he would.

Winnie spun toward the door, as if she was going to leave.

"Woah there. Where do you think you're going?" Gavin asked, moving quickly toward her.

"To figure things out," she answered, glancing over her shoulder.

Without thinking, Gavin reached out and grabbed her arm. He pulled her to him.

Winnie gasped, and backed up. "What are you doing?"

"Trying to distract you. Make you forget what you were talking about. I was about to kiss you," he admitted. After all, that's what she'd done to him. Only…she didn't look flustered at his suggestion. Or pink-cheeked. Or any of those things that she'd been the last time when she'd kissed him.

He frowned. Had he done something wrong? She was glaring at him and not the least bit distracted. Well, maybe she was? He didn't want to kiss her without asking, that's why he hadn't.

"It's not going to work." She crossed her arms.

Might as well be truthful. "I had hoped it would. You tried it on me." He crossed his arms as well.

"Yes, well..." She flushed.

Gavin fixed her with a hard look. "You're going to sneak away, aren't you? Try and do this on your own. There's a much easier solution. You could still pretend to be my wife."

As he waited for the words to sink in, he couldn't help but feel the melancholy that those words held. He knew once he helped her and she was reunited with her siblings, that would be it. She wouldn't return to Red Ridge. And that meant he'd likely never see her again.

But he was sheriff. Had pledged to help all those in his town who needed him, and without personal gain. Even before he'd taken the badge, he knew there would be sacrifices he'd have to make. He just hadn't realized until this very moment how difficult some of them would be.

* * *

"You've got to let one of us join you," Billy said. His brow was furrowed. "Who knows what you're walking into. You can't do this on your own."

"I'll have Ryan," Gavin said, stuffing clothes into a bag. He glanced around and reached into a box where he kept a little extra money, and put that in too.

"It's not the same," Billy said, his tone harsh. "He's a tracker. Not a gun. He won't have your back like we would."

Gavin turned and faced him, then put a hand on Billy's shoulder. "I know it's not the same," he said. "There's nobody I want more than you and Eli with me."

Eli stood nearby, simply listening. Gavin looked between his friends, and wasn't at all embarrassed that his words caught for a moment. "But I'm counting on you both. Someone's got to look after the town. You've both got wives. Billy, you just finally got Mirabelle. Hannah's got a babe on the way. If something…If this is the time that…I just can't risk you. I can't do that to them."

Eli stepped forward, clapped Billy on the shoulder, and then did the same to Gavin. "There won't be a risk. You'll be in and out," he said. "Slick and slippery. Like that time in Arizona."

"That's right," Gavin said. They'd snuck in and gotten out, taking the bounty with them before any alarm could be raised. He shrugged as he checked his gun. "Besides, I have to be careful. Winnie is coming along."

Billy's eyebrows shot up. "Winnie? So that's the real reason you don't want us, huh?" He started to laugh. "Winnie, huh? Since when did you two get on a first-name basis?"

"Shut it," Gavin growled, and turned back to his packing. He regretted the moment of feeling sentimental.

From the corner of his eye, he saw Eli give Billy a look, and Billy wiped that stupid grin off his face. Gavin was glad. If it'd been on there much longer, he might have smacked it off himself.

"All right. So, you and Ryan. I'm sure you'll have a good plan for the rescue. What happens after you get the kids?" Eli asked.

His somber eyes met Gavin's, and he realized his friend knew his worry even though he hadn't said it out loud. "I don't know," he said quietly. "I guess she'll settle somewhere with her siblings."

His friends didn't say anything, but their serious faces told him they were not only worried about him leaving, but also about the possibility of him coming back alone.

Wordlessly, they helped him finish packing, and Eli reminded him as he mounted his horse, "Send word if you need help. Nothing will keep me away. I'll be there faster than anything."

"Same," Billy said. "I'm always ready to ride in and save my best friend."

The lump came back into Gavin's throat, and he nodded. He couldn't say anything. He didn't have to. They'd been together so much, Eli and Billy knew what was in his heart and likely even how it was feeling right now. Gavin waved and rode hard, heading into town. The stage left in an hour.

As the wind hit his face, he tried to let it blow away his worries, but no matter how he wanted to lose himself in the soothing rhythm of his mare's hooves and pretend everything was fine, he knew it wasn't. These might be the final hours he got to spend with Winnie.

Or alive.

Chapter 16

Wearily, Winnie climbed from the stagecoach, allowing Gavin to assist her. The ride to meet his friend and rescue her sister and brother had been bumpy, overfilled with passengers, and her legs felt cramped. Though now standing, her achy body still felt as though she was jolting along. It would take a while for her to recover, though her comfort was the last thing on her mind.

The entire trip, she'd only had two thoughts. First, her siblings. The second, that Gavin was incredibly kind and attentive. For the last two days, he'd seen to her every need or comfort. From getting her food and drink, to glaring at any of the men who tried to encroach upon her limited space. At stops, he bought her a newspaper or a book, some sweets, and once, a flower. She'd been grateful for the flower, and kept it close to her nose to mask the scent of some of the passengers.

While she hadn't asked for a thing, he seemed to anticipate her every need. Winnie hadn't argued or tried to stop his gestures. As they were pretending to be married, it would have looked odd if she'd argued with him about paying for something.

Madge and Lisa had been very understanding when she'd explained the situation and apologized for leaving. They told her to hurry back, and Winnie promised she would. She wondered, though, would she? Would her siblings be willing to move to that town? How would she provide for them? They couldn't all stay in her room at the boarding house. And would she even want to go back? Could her heart let her? She enjoyed her job, but could she live there in Red Ridge seeing Gavin, and—

"He should be here," Gavin said, pulling her from her thoughts. He looked around the crowd. "I just—" He suddenly waved, and took her hand, leading her through the crowd.

At his touch, Winnie had startled, but then she remembered it was allowed. No one knew they weren't truly married. Gavin had told her the only way she'd be going with him, and for her own safety, was as a married woman, ersatz marriage or real.

But what would happen once she had her siblings and they went on their way? The question had been in her mind on their trip. There was no reason for her to return to Red Ridge. Yes, she had a job, but she could get one anywhere. There wasn't anything there waiting for her to return to it.

But...deep within, Winnie knew that wasn't true. Gavin had made it plain he was interested in her. He'd also not pressed her for a reply. As they'd traveled, and his sharp gaze never relaxed, Winnie had felt sure of one thing. She was going to miss him when the time came and they parted ways. She didn't think she'd ever felt so safe or so special to someone.

If she was to be truthful, she didn't want to be without him. But soon she'd be responsible for her siblings. That meant giving them her focus, care, and attention. She had to make it up to them. There was no way she could think about herself, and what she might want. Who she might want. She owed it to them.

They stopped suddenly in front of a lanky man, just a little younger than Gavin with dark hair that curled. The man grabbed Gavin, who let out a shout and returned the hug.

"Ryan Lundy," Gavin said, the grin coming through in his voice. "It's good to see you." His tone sobered. "Though I wish it were under better circumstances, I appreciate your swift arrival and help."

"I'd have come regardless," Ryan said, "but my life is yours. After what happened in Wyoming, I don't think I can ever repay you."

"Not needed," Gavin said. "I've told you that. Having my friend alive is all I need."

He looked at Winnie, and said, "This is Winnie, their sister."

"Ma'am," Ryan said politely, taking her hand and shaking it. "Have a good trip?"

"As well as can be," she told him. "I want to add my own thanks. I appreciate you helping me locate my siblings."

"I just wish they weren't in such a place," he said, his eyes darkening, "and that you hadn't lost the man after them."

"As do I," Winnie said quietly.

"Let's get a bite and talk things over," Ryan said.

"Why can't we go to them now?" Winnie asked.

"Because I need to tell Gavin everything I've learned," Ryan told her. "I understand you are anxious to see your siblings, but an hour or two's planning might be the thing that saves their lives. They aren't in a good situation, but they are safe and secure for right now."

Reluctantly, she nodded. He was right. Though she wanted to rush toward the ghastly building where her siblings were being held, it would likely get them hurt or herself captured. She had to be calm. Reasonable. Let the men who'd done this before lead the way and do what they did best.

"There's a place just ahead," Ryan said. "Ate there last night and still alive."

Winnie blanched, but then quickly realized it was a joke. They set off, and Gavin and Ryan kept their conversation light. He was filling them in on Eli and Billy. Winnie was curious; she'd not seen either of the other gunslingers around the town yet.

When they arrived at the café, Gavin held the door for her, then pulled out the chair of a corner table.

"Never thought I'd see this," Ryan said, gesturing between her and Gavin. "Gavin's the best man I know, though. Makes me happy to see you again, and settling down. You make a good couple. Congratulations."

Winnie felt guilty at the lie, and glanced at Gavin. He winked at her, and that made her smile.

Ryan stood. "Back in a moment," he said, and left the table.

"I feel terrible lying," Winnie whispered as he left. "He's such a nice man. Wouldn't he keep our secret?"

"He would," Gavin agreed, "but I'm being selfish."

"What do you mean?" Winnie asked.

He shrugged and winked at her. "I've done plenty of pretending in my gunslinging days."

She stiffened. Had he been with other women so many times that pretending to be married came naturally to him? Jealousy, though she knew she shouldn't have it, flooded her.

"That said," Gavin continued, "I've never pretended to be married before. I don't want to tell anyone it's not real. They might try to steal you."

Relief washed over her, as well as pleasure, but to hide it, she teased, "Is that so? What do you think about marriage? Ready to run away yet?"

Then, her cheeks turned pink as he leaned close and whispered, "I like it. But only because it's you."

Ryan came back just then, and the food not a minute later. Winnie was delighted that the meal was more than passable, it was delicious. She ate a chicken pot pie and listened as the friends caught up.

"One day, when we have time, I'll tell you some stories about Gavin," Ryan said, as he winked at her.

"And I'll tell you ones about him," Gavin said, a brow raised. "He's an excellent tracker, and there's no exaggeration in any tale with him in it."

"Same with you," Ryan said. "We're a good team. I am going to have to visit this Red Ridge place you run now, say hello to Billy and Eli."

"Any time," Gavin said. "You'd be more than welcome."

Ryan sighed, "As much as I want to relive the old days, it's time for business." He set his fork down. "Let me tell you what I've found out since I got here."

Winnie's stomach churned, and she wished she'd not eaten so much. Gavin seemed to sense her distress, and reached over and held her hand. "It's going to be okay," he told her, squeezing her hand gently. "This is what we do."

"It is," Ryan said, giving her a reassuring smile. Then, he nodded at Gavin, his expression now one of all business. "There's a two-story saloon a few buildings down. The girl's being kept in one of the rooms upstairs. Far as I know, she's not entertained any clients yet. Only arrived about two weeks ago. Before that, she'd been a saloon girl. She was so bad at serving, they decided to use her elsewhere."

Gavin nodded. "Anyone on the inside to help us out?"

"No. Can't get anyone," Ryan said. "It's just us, and going in blind. Haven't been able to get eyes in the room I think she's in. I do have a set of skeleton keys though. Should open any door she's behind."

"Then that's what we will do," Gavin said. "Won't be the first time we went in without enough information. The boy?"

"He's been doing small jobs. The plan is to train him to be a thief or cheat at cards." Ryan drank from his mug. "When I saw him, he looked healthy, if a little scrawny."

"Good. You and I will stop in the saloon," Gavin started.

"What about me?" Winnie asked. "What will I do?"

"Stay here. You can't go with us." Gavin was firm.

"But why?" She tried not to raise her voice, but anger filled her. "They are my siblings."

"And you are a woman. Women don't go into saloons unless they are working there." Gavin raised his brows and waited for his words to sink in.

"Oh." Her cheeks colored.

Ryan added, "It will be less obvious with two men going to a saloon than a woman and a man, or a woman and two men." He glanced at Gavin. "You going to let local law know?"

"I thought about that," Gavin said, and rubbed his jaw. "But I don't think so. I don't know if he can be trusted, if he'll take too long to show up, and if he is going to make things take too long with all the paperwork. The kids are there, and I don't want to wait."

"I agree," Ryan said. "I expect it's a lot harder for you now. Having to do things by the rules."

Gavin nodded. "That's why we have to be quiet and quick. The plan is to sneak them out, and no one will know."

"How will you do that?" Winnie asked. She hadn't thought about the fact he was risking both his job and his reputation as a man to uphold the law by helping her. When would the guilt she felt over others helping her—and paying for it—end?

Gavin grinned and drummed his fingers on the table. "I'm going to do what I do best. Make things up as I go."

Chapter 17

Winnie had not been happy being told to stay put at the hotel room Ryan had secured for them. Gavin understood why. They were her siblings, and she was worried about them. She also hadn't seen them for a long time. However, he'd been correct in the fact that reputable women couldn't go inside a saloon, even just to look around.

He'd finally left her, under the impression she'd be watching through the window. That was about as good as he was going to get, and he knew if circumstances were switched, he wouldn't have been able to sit still either.

The sooner they found the kids, the better. He and Ryan tried not to draw attention to themselves as they walked to the saloon doors and, with a small nod at each other, walked through. The plan was to go inside, get a good look at the area, and then split up. Gavin was to look for the girl, Ryan the boy.

As they walked inside, the smell of smoke and spirits hit his nose. A piano was playing slightly off key near the back of the room, and the place was filled with men. There was loud talking and laughter, and a scuffle in the back corner. It was perfect. There was so much going on, it wouldn't be noticed if they slipped away.

A few scantily clad women served drinks or hovered near the gaming table. They were all smiles and teasing touches. Gavin knew they'd be telling their favorite players the others' cards with secret gestures. It might be a saloon he'd never been inside, but all were pretty similar in what they offered and what they contained.

He and Ryan went to the bar and sat down on the worn stools just as two men got up. They wrapped their hands around the men's discarded cups, pretending they were their own. This would save them from having to order. Neither of them were one for a strong drink. In this line of work, it was important to keep a clear head, fast reflexes, and sharp eyes.

Gavin let his eyes follow a man laughing loudly as he walked up the stairs, a woman with a red dress and bare shoulders on his arm. He wondered how many people were up there. Would he be able to search for Winnie's sister without bumping into someone?

It was likely Lily was upstairs, unless she'd been moved since Ryan was there last. However, there were far too many doors to just go up and start opening them. Besides, they'd all be locked. Not that the locks were a problem, but he didn't want to waste time or get caught.

Ryan had been here the night before, and before they came to the saloon, told him all he knew about the various doors and where they led. There was a small room that connected back behind the bar, likely a storeroom, and another that was off to the side.

As Gavin was scanning the area, a large man came out from the door, crossed his arms, and stood watching the crowd. Gavin wondered if he ran the saloon or the criminal activities.

Ryan walked over to the piano and dropped some money in trade for a rousing tune that got half the room dancing. Gavin used everyone getting up to disguise himself moving up the stairs. He hurriedly moved down the hallway. There were a half dozen doors on each side.

However, he easily found the room Ryan had told him about. Last on the right. He just hoped the information his friend had gotten was correct and that Winnie's sister was inside. If she'd been moved somewhere else, he wasn't sure where to start looking.

Someone approached. He barely heard them over the ruckus below, but he spun and his fingers were at his belt before he had time to stop himself. Just as he brought his gun up, he saw Ryan and dropped his hand. Gavin glanced over his friend's shoulder. Still clear. He jerked his thumb at the door while raising his brows, and Ryan nodded.

Gavin tried the knob. Locked, as he figured it would be. He was reaching for the skeleton key set he'd brought, when he noticed the lock. His keys were too large.

"That's new," Ryan said. "Wasn't there last night when I was walking around."

"Going to take a moment," Gavin said as he inspected the lock.

He reached inside of his jacket and pulled out a few tools and set to work. He took his time, even though he knew that wasn't something he had. At any moment someone could spot them. Or the door could open from the inside. He couldn't let himself get rattled, though. That was when a mistake might happen. Gavin didn't want anything to happen to Winnie's siblings, and he sure didn't want himself or Ryan to get hurt.

Calmly, he worked the picks, refusing to let himself rush or panic, even though he wondered who might be behind the door. A moment later, a small click rewarded him, and the lock opened. Gavin pocketed the lock and the tool.

There hadn't been any noise they could hear from inside the room, but it was also difficult to make out anything overtop the offkey singing of "Sweet Betsy from Pike."

Ryan was humming along and tapping his foot. When Gavin raised a brow, he just grinned. "Looking the part, my friend. You have to admit, though, it's a good song."

Not answering, Gavin pushed open the door to the room. It was a large corner room. Immediately, he saw a bed, a table, and a chair. There was a whimper, and he turned in the direction, gun pointed at the sound. Three girls wearing only their chemises were clinging to each other with terrified faces. He and Ryan hurried in and closed the door behind them.

"We aren't here to hurt you," Gavin said, keeping his eyes only on their faces to try and reassure them. "I'm looking for a girl named Lily and her brother Nick."

One of the girls, the one who looked to be oldest, whispered, "I'm Lily. But I don't know where my brother is. Who are you?"

"Your sister sent me," Gavin told her. "Are you hurt? Are any of you hurt?"

The girls shook their heads, and the other two crowded around him right away.

"You'll help us?" one asked. "Are you the sheriff?"

"I want to go home," the third sobbed, grabbing at him.

"Shh," Lily scolded, a short distance from the others. "We have to be quiet." She looked at Gavin then. "How do I know my sister sent you? What's her name?"

"Winnie," he answered. "Winifred Anderson."

Her eyes narrowed, and he caught a spark of the fire Winnie had. "Any other proof?"

"Ah..." Gavin glanced at Ryan, who shrugged. "Well, she's quick to scowl. Hair the color of yours. Can't stop feeling guilty about getting a job and—"

"Good enough," Lily said. "What's the plan?"

Gavin tried not to smile. He liked her no-nonsense way. He wondered if Nick was going to be the same. The Anderson siblings obviously were sharp minded and quick thinkers.

"We're going to sneak out," Ryan said. He glanced at the girls. "You aren't quite dressed like saloon girls, but we're going to have to make it work."

"What do you mean?" Lily asked.

"No way down but the stairs and the main door," Gavin said grimly, "unless you go through the window, and we don't have rope."

"Then that's what we have to do," Lily said. "Down the stairs it is." She glanced down at herself. "But not in this."

"Are there any clothes in here?" Ryan asked, scanning the room.

"Over here." Lily ran across to a wardrobe. When she pulled it open, bright silk dresses greeted the men.

"We'll put these on," Lily said. "Then we'll blend in." She started to distribute the dresses.

"You've got to hurry," Gavin warned.

The girls threw the clothes on, helping each other button the backs, then silently waited, nervous looks on their faces as they looked at Gavin and Ryan. The dresses were a poor fit. Meant for fully grown women, they were loose in spots, but hopefully no one would notice.

Gavin quietly said, "Lily, you come with me. I've got to have my gun hand free. Stay on this side."

"Same," Ryan said. "One on my arm, the other right behind me."

"Maybe…carry something," Gavin said to the third girl, who was standing there nervously. His eyes darted around the room. "Then you might blend in better." He spotted a tray with some glasses and motioned to it.

The girl took it, nodding with a confidence her eyes didn't possess.

"Let's go," Gavin said. He cracked open the door and peered into the hallway. The piano's loud banging of "Paddy Works on the Railway" filled his ears, and he motioned to others in the room.

"Billy sure loves this song," Ryan said, his head nodding along. "Remember when you played it for us in California?"

"The easy days," Gavin snorted. With Lily's hand firmly in his, Gavin moved toward the stairs. He fully intended to rescue all of the girls, but Lily was his main concern. He had to get her out quietly, too, as they still had to find the boy. He'd have to come back and poke around. There was no help for it, but the longer it took, the easier they could be caught. Especially if someone noticed the three girls missing.

The song slowed as they got to the top of the stairs, then the crowd burst out into the next verse, clapping and stomping, nearly shouting the lyrics. Gavin and Ryan sang along as loudly as they could, stumbling toward the door with the girls.

"In eighteen hundred and forty-four, I landed on Columbia's shore, I landed upon Columbia's shore, to work upon the railway," everyone roared in the saloon.

A woman carrying a tray of drinks approached them, looking puzzled when she saw the girls on their arms. Ryan released the two he was leading out, took the saloon woman into his arms, and spun her around, leading her into the middle of the crowd.

The large man Gavin had spotted before was near the bar, talking to the man behind the bar with a serious expression. Gavin wondered what they were discussing, as the man thumbed toward the door he'd come out of earlier.

Shouting the chorus and waving an empty glass in the air, Gavin pushed all the girls toward the door. "In eighteen hundred and forty-six, I changed my trade to carrying bricks, I changed my trade to carrying bricks, from working on the railway," he howled, as he sang the crowd's obviously favorite song.

The saloon was shaking so hard from the stomping, Gavin thought it a wonder that the whole building hadn't collapsed by now. It was clear that the loud noise didn't alarm the town, as no one came to check to quiet the saloon.

He'd just gotten the girls out and pushed around the side of the building when something caught his eye. A familiar woman, the expression on her face one of determination, slipped inside the saloon. Gavin's jaw tightened, and he started after her, just as Ryan came through the doors.

"Take the girls to safety," Gavin growled as he pushed past, gun in hand. "I don't know why, but Winnie just went inside."

Chapter 18

Winnie didn't quite know what to expect when she went inside the saloon, but it sure wasn't a room full of people singing at the top of their lungs, glasses splashing amber liquids everywhere, and people dancing around bumping into each other while the card players didn't even look up from their hands.

The place also stunk. There was no other word for it. Between the heavy smoke from cigars and the unwashed bodies all clustered together, she felt a little sick. Why in the world would people want to come to a place like this, she wondered.

She thought she'd seen Gavin and Ryan hustling her sister out, and hoped that her eyes weren't playing tricks on her. She'd seen them with three girls, anyway. As much as she wanted to check on Lily, or who she hoped was

Lily, she knew Nick was the one who needed her most. Hopefully, she wasn't too late. And, also hopefully, Gavin would understand why she'd come here, even though he was right—it was no place for her.

But there was no choice. Not after what she'd overheard. In the hotel, she'd gone down to the small restaurant to order some tea and sit near the window to watch Gavin. It was perfectly situated right across the street and at an angle from the saloon. She had a good view, and kept her eyes focused on the window.

After she'd finished her second cup of tea, a large man had come in and approached two men sitting at the table behind her. Winnie pretended to be absorbed in her book, but it hadn't escaped her attention the first man had come from the saloon.

"The kid tried to get to his sister again," the man had growled. "So I tied him up. He's trouble. This is the third time."

"Get rid of him," the second man said calmly. "He won't be any good to us. We don't need him anyway. He was just a bonus."

The man had left with a grunt, and walked back into the saloon. While it was true, Winnie didn't know for a fact that the men were talking about Lily and Nick, she had a strong suspicion that's who they were referencing. After all, how many other brothers and sisters could there be in that exact saloon? To be sure, that wasn't a common occurrence—at least she didn't imagine it was.

As calmly as she could, she waited until the man had crossed the street, then she counted to two hundred and slowly rose, pretending as if she hadn't a care in the world, while leaving money on the table.

She returned to her room, dropped her book on the bed, and then paced furiously. What to do? There was only one thing, and that was to help Nick. But how? She wasn't sure on that part, and hoped it came to her.

Biting her lip, she hurried near the saloon. She heard loud singing and a moment later, two men with three young women wearing dresses that were much too large for them hustled out and around the corner.

She recognized Gavin, but it had only been him and Ryan. No Nick. Her heart dropped. They must not have found him. She was sure he'd found Lily, though. Even though there had only been a flash of her, Winnie sensed it.

Winnie ignored the thumping of fear in her heart. There was no help for it. She had to try. If that man was about to kill her brother, she had no choice but to find Nick and free him. It was her responsibility. He was her responsibility. And it was her who would live with the pain and the guilt if she didn't at least try.

Though she knew Gavin would be angry at her if he knew what she was about to do, fear for her brother overcame everything else. She'd be a willing sacrifice if that meant her brother would be safe.

Winnie slipped inside the saloon. Every moment mattered. But now, she stood, uncertain what she should do. Perhaps she should have approached Gavin, told him what she'd overheard? But it was too late. She didn't know where he was.

Winnie tried to blend against the wall as a tired looking woman walked past her. "Don't just stand there. Clear those cups," she snapped, shoving a tray at Winnie. "Lazy girl!"

Startled, but glad for the excuse to hide as an employee, Winnie accepted the tray, and slowly worked her way around the room. But where should she go to find Nick?

The large man she'd seen at the hotel walked past her then, opened a door, and started inside.

"Jim!" the bartender yelled. The man stopped. "Come 'ere. Boss wants ya."

The man closed the door, but not before Winnie caught the flash of a teenage boy tied to a chair. She swiftly headed that way, picking up empty glasses as she went and loading her tray. The door hadn't quite closed and she pushed it open, then set down her tray, hastily closing the door behind her.

"Nick?" she asked, her voice trembling. Her eyes searched his face, wondering if he'd recognize her. "Are you hurt?"

"Winnie!" Nick gasped as he stared at her. "Is it really you?" Then, he spoke urgently. "They've got Lily. She's upstairs, but I don't know where. There's a bunch of rooms." He struggled against the ropes, and the chair thumped.

"She's okay," Winnie assured him as she turned and looked at the closed door behind them. She searched for something heavy to put against it while she freed Nick, but there wasn't anything.

"A friend got her out. Now, we need to get you. A man is on his way to..." She didn't want to finish her sentence, but Nick nodded, like he knew.

"I wouldn't help them," he told her. "And I kept trying to get to Lily, to get her back when they took her." His voice caught. "I tried, Winnie. I tried."

"Shh, my dear, I know you did," Winnie said soothingly. "We're all together again. At least, we will be once we get out of here. We have to hurry, though. I don't know how long we have."

"It won't be long," Nick answered. "He's coming back to get rid of me. You better go. Just help Lily before they take you too."

"I will not. I will not just leave you," Winnie scolded him. "We go together."

She knew neither of them wanted to die that day, but it was a distinct possibility. She desperately hoped a miracle would happen, and the three of them would escape. Winnie also knew that, like herself, her brother would sacrifice himself if he needed to. The two of them were very similar in their stubbornness. But she refused to let that happen.

The thought of the detective came to her mind, and a wave of guilt washed over Winnie. He was another she was responsible for. His death was on her hands. She'd sent an innocent man to be slaughtered. Her guilt may never lessen.

"Winnie?"

She startled, bringing her thoughts back to the present, and moved behind her brother, wishing she had something to cut the ropes that tied him. She tugged, but they were tight. Was there anything that could help her? Biting her lip, she glanced around.

"Do you have a pocket knife?" Winnie asked as she picked at the knot.

"No. They took it," Nick said. "How'd you get here? How'd you find us?"

"That's a long story," Winnie said. She gently tugged here and pulled there and was relieved to feel the knot loosen a little. She continued to work at it. "When I got to the town I was sent to by the woman I worked for, there happened to be a sheriff. When I explained to him I was worried because neither you nor Lily had contacted me when you got out of the orphanage, he offered to help me find you."

She grunted as she worked at the rope. "And here we are."

"Lily wasn't sixteen before she was took," Nick said.

"Taken," Winnie corrected automatically. Then froze. "Wait, what do you mean?"

"I mean, we got sold by someone at the orphanage. A bunch of us. At first, we went to some place where we sewed all the time. Then one day a man walked in, caught sight of Lily, and tried to take her. I told him we were a package deal. Don't know why, but he agreed, and that's how we ended up here."

"I see," Winnie said. The knot wouldn't loosen any more. She didn't know what to do, but knew deep within her time was almost out. Maybe her teeth? She bent over the knot and chewed at it.

"When we got here, that's when we found out. Lily and two other girls he took were going to be..." He stopped, stiffening like he was uncomfortable to talk further.

"It's okay," Winnie said. "I know. And if this horrid rope would just—"

She broke off as the door started to open. Panicked, Winnie looked around.

There was nowhere to hide.

Chapter 19

Gavin strode into the saloon like he hadn't just danced out of it minutes before. His eyes cooly took in the room as he sought Winnie. It was much as he'd left it. Singing, dancing, drinking, gambling.

But Winnie...she wasn't anywhere around. If he hadn't been so concerned, he'd have been furious. The only reason he wasn't was because he knew something was wrong. Could feel it deep inside him.

The large man he'd seen earlier was at the bar, and Gavin drifted closer. The man smacked at the bar and looked angry, and Gavin wanted to know why. Maybe he could overhear something that would help him.

"Found the boss at the hotel restaurant. Says finish the kid off," the man said. "I guess we, what, just leave his body until everyone's gone? Don't know what he expects me to do with it."

"Why'd he even bring the kid? Was trouble from day one. Always trying to get to his sister," the barkeeper said, shaking his head. "Just do it quiet like. Or leave him for later. Don't need the sheriff coming by. Nobody knows who Nick is, and he's got no family but his sister, so won't nobody be looking for him."

Gavin tried not to let it show he was listening. His heart sped up a little, though. This must be why Winnie was here. She'd also overheard. He took a deep breath. He could find her, and the boy. There was time. He just needed to figure out where they were.

He eased himself toward the card table, grabbing a nearly empty cup someone had abandoned. You stood out less in a saloon if you were holding something.

The man at the bar downed a drink and walked toward the room Gavin had seen him leave from earlier. The man walked in, then froze. What was he staring at? Gavin inched closer, and tried to see.

Just then, one of the card players threw down his cards and pulled out his gun. Gavin dove to the side as a brawl started, with men punching and kicking. There were screams of the female variety, but there were saloon girls around, so Gavin couldn't tell if one of the shrieks had come from Winnie.

By the time he'd gotten over to the door, a prayer on his lips he wasn't too late to get the kid, the room had gone back to loud laughter and music, and the card players had settled back down.

The only thing that changed faster than the mood in a saloon was the weather in Texas.

Gavin cracked the door open, then pushed in, gun out. A teenager was tied to a chair and glared at him the moment he came in. "Here to finish me off?" he growled.

"Nope." Holstering his gun, Gavin pulled out a knife. The boy swallowed, but met his gaze dead on. "You Nick?" he asked. The boy nodded. "Good. My name's Gavin. I came with Winnie."

"They took her," Nick blurted. He used his head to gesture the way Gavin had just come from.

"What? Who?" Gavin sawed at the ropes.

"The man who was going to kill me. He grabbed Winnie. He'll be back," Nick said, and stood once the ropes were off him. "I'll be ready, though," he added, jaw jutting out.

If Gavin hadn't been so worried about Winnie, he'd have stopped to remark on the expression on Nick's face. He'd seen it on Winnie's, as well. A smile quirked all the same. It was obvious they were related. Fire filled all three of the Anderson siblings. A determination to look after each other too.

"Tell me where he took her," Gavin said, handing the boy his knife and pulling back out his gun.

"Upstairs," Nick said. "I'm going with you." He spun the blade, then grabbed the handle firmly.

Gavin looked on in approval. The boy might have some skills. But facts were facts. He was Winnie's brother, and Gavin liked being alive. He couldn't let him go.

"No. You're getting outside, and to the creek behind the saloon. My friend is there, with your other sister. If you get hurt, Winnie will kill me," Gavin said. "Likely you next."

Nick barked a short laugh. "She might. She's scarier than these guys," he agreed. "I wouldn't want to be on her bad side. Okay. I'm going to check on Lily. But if you take long, I'm coming back in."

He started toward the door, then stopped. All trace of humor was gone from his face, and his eyes made Gavin think of Eli's boring into him. They had that same deep look, one where a thousand things were said silently. "You get her," Nick said. "Bring her back to us. Lily and I—we need her."

"I do too," Gavin said quietly to himself as the kid left, hoping he'd get a chance to tell Winnie that. He peered around the corner, and just in time to see a flash of Winnie at the top of the stairs, struggling.

Gavin ran after her. The only thought in his mind was her safety. He would get to her, help her, and nothing else mattered. Not his own life, not even those kids. Ryan would care for them. Could find his way back to Eli and Billy, if things came to it. But Winnie... He had to protect her.

He'd known it for a while now, he loved her. She might not feel the same way, he wasn't really sure, but regardless, he'd either live out the rest of his days knowing that he'd protected her and rescued her siblings, or he'd die trying.

He wasn't far away now. He could see Winnie and the man who had grabbed her arm and was twisting it.

"Could use another woman for the saloon," he said, smirking. "Perk of the job, I get to sample all of them myself first. If you become my favorite, I'll treat you well."

"Never. I'll throw myself out of this window first," Winnie hissed.

"You say that," the man agreed, "but soon as you start dangling, you'll change your mind."

"I won't," Winnie said. "Don't you dare touch me."

The man laughed. He laughed so hard he put a hand on his stomach and nearly doubled over. Gavin was creeping closer. He wanted to shoot, but didn't want to hit Winnie. She was too close, and she was also unpredictable. He wouldn't put it past her to—

Yep. She did it. Walked right into his line of sight. He huffed out a breath softly, and crept closer. There wasn't a clear shot, so he'd have to make one.

"You disgust me," Winnie said, and slapped the man.

The man lunged for her, but she pulled away. He still managed to grab hold of her around her middle, and Winnie struggled, shrieking something unintelligible. Her hands swung, and one connected with the man's nose. He roared, and spun her, shoving her headfirst through the window.

Winnie half dangled, half struggled as the man laughed. "This is what you wanted," he said. "Fine by me. There are plenty more women. Everyone's replaceable."

"Let her go." Gavin stood, sights firmly on the man in front of him.

The man glanced over at him. "A hero, huh? Don't think so. She's mine, to do with whatever I want. Even this. Won't no one stop me."

"That's where you're wrong," Gavin said. An incredible wave of peace washed over him. Focus. Calm. Winnie was so far through the window he couldn't see but her bottom half, but she had stilled. Knew he was there. Maybe even knew this was goodbye.

There was the sound of firearms cocking behind him, and Gavin didn't risk turning around to see if they belonged to friend or foe. In a place like this, he doubted it was a friend. It didn't matter, though. He'd protect her, even with his last breath.

Steel filled Gavin's voice. "She's not yours. She's mine."

The next sound was a shot that blasted his ears.

Chapter 20

At the gunshot, Winnie froze. She was scared to move. Scared to look. The last thing she'd heard before that shot was Gavin's voice. Was that going to be the last time she ever heard it?

Her hands were clinging to the small window ledge as she tried to hold on. The man gripping her let go. Shouts and more shooting came from below in the saloon, along with a few screams, before there was an eerie silence.

Slowly, Winnie closed her eyes. Fear filled every inch of her. She'd been a fool. Had wasted too much time. Time when she should have admitted to herself and to him that she was falling in love with him. And now? It was too late. He'd rescued her sister. Tried to save her. Nick too. He'd risked his all, and she'd never told him thank you. Never said what she should have. That she appreciated him. That she loved him.

Hands touched her, gently, but still she flinched. There was a roaring sound in her ears, and Winnie started to struggle. Her legs kicked backward.

"It's me, it's me," Gavin's voice, close to her, said.

Winnie let out a cry as she tried to wriggle back into the saloon. She let him pull her back through the window, then wrapped her arms around him. "Gavin," she said, holding him tightly, her face buried in his chest. Her voice rose with fear, but she didn't pull away. "I'm so sorry. They were going to kill Nick. I had to!" She sobbed, then cried out, "My brother! I must find him."

"I know," he said soothingly, arms holding her close. "It's okay. Everyone's okay. Lily is safe, and so is Nick. I got to him in time."

She didn't release him. Didn't want to be let go. His words made her relax. Nick was safe. Gavin was safe. But... Just a fraction, Winnie moved her head to see his face. "Are...are you hurt?" she choked out. "I heard the shot and..."

"I'm fine," he assured her. Reluctantly, he pulled back. "It was me. I shot first. I didn't want to, and he's still alive, but I had to. I'd best let the local sheriff know."

"Already did," a man's voice said.

Winnie looked over. She didn't recognize the man standing next to Gavin's friend Ryan, but based on the surprised expression on his face, Gavin did.

"Eli?" Gavin shook his head. He released her and walked to the man. "You're here. How?"

"Felt I needed to be," Eli said. His eyes swept the hallway. "You good?"

"Better than." Gavin grinned as he clapped him on the shoulder.

"Knew you'd need us," another man chirped, sticking his head out of a room. "All clear. No one upstairs."

Gavin pulled him in for a hug. "Billy! You fool. Mirabelle is going to be mad at me. Hannah too."

Hannah? Mirabelle? Winnie looked at the men with open curiosity. These must be the husbands of the women she'd met in the general store, and Gavin's closest friends. Winnie could sense their bond, and felt tears form in her eyes that they'd dropped everything to help him. She worried, though, that the two women might resent her for it later.

"Ah, no," Billy said, turning so red the tips of his ears pinked. "Mirabelle told me if I didn't go after you and help Winnie, well, I best not come home for supper ever again." He glanced at her. "Hello. Nice to meet you. Mirabelle said to invite you and Gavin for dinner on Thursday."

"Hannah said something along those lines too," Eli said, and tipped his hat at her. "Also, our place, Saturday evening. She's making fried chicken, since it's your favorite, Gavin. Wants to know Winnie better." He squinted around the hallway. "Glad we got here before it was over. It was all I could do to keep Gus from coming."

Gavin laughed at that.

Winnie didn't know who Gus was, but hoped to meet him soon. Her heart also felt lighter, that the two women she'd met weren't upset at her, but instead, had insisted their husbands come, and had extended invitations to get to know her better.

"That's what I wanted to do," Eli agreed mildly. "But I insisted he protect the women. As we rode off, they had him in the middle, and he was preening something fierce."

Just then, the man who'd grabbed her let out a groan and tried to crawl away. Blood was staining the arm of his shirt. Gavin stopped him and hauled him to his feet. "Don't think so."

"Please, just let me go," the man begged. "Take her and leave. I don't care."

"After kidnapping and threatening? I can't do that," Gavin said. "Got to do some things by the book."

"Sure do," a man with a star pinned to his chest said. "And I've been looking for a reason to put this man away. Good job, Sheriff Jefferson."

"Thank you," Gavin said, reaching out. "I apologize I didn't alert you I was in town, Sheriff. Wasn't expecting to find trouble."

"Finds us when we least expect it," the sheriff said. "I'm Sheriff Taylor. Your friend, Ryan Lundy, came and got me. Told me those kids and your woman were kidnapped. Sorry I wasn't here sooner, but looks like you had a little backup."

Gavin's arm wrapped around her, and Winnie didn't miss the pride in his voice as he nodded at Eli and Billy. "The best kind."

"I'll get a statement from you later," the sheriff said, then left with the prisoner in tow.

"It's gotten real quiet," Billy said. "Shame. That was my favorite song they were playing. Wonder if the pianist is still downstairs."

Eli shrugged. "We broke up the fun. But I agree. Like that one. Reminds me of that time in California."

Gavin chuckled. "Ryan and I were just saying that earlier. I'll have to play it later for us." He glanced at her. "Ready to see Lily and Nick?"

"I thought you'd never ask." Winnie smiled so wide her cheeks ached.

He led her out of the saloon, but didn't let go of her hand. There, right outside of the now-quiet building, Lily and Nick waited. When they saw her, they rushed at her, hugging her tightly. Happy tears sprang from Winnie's eyes as she hugged and kissed and held her siblings. It felt so good to be reunited. Winnie vowed to never be away from them again.

A short distance away, Gavin stood back, watching them as he talked quietly to his friends.

Lily stepped away from the hug first. She glanced at Gavin, and asked, "Winnie, who is that?"

Taking her hand, Winnie walked closer to him. "Lily, Nick, this is Gavin. He is the man..." she stopped. What was she to say?

"Who wants to marry her," Gavin finished. He held out his hand for them to shake. "Gavin Jefferson, gunslinger and sheriff of Red Ridge."

"I've heard of you," Nick blurted. "But how can a gunslinger also be a sheriff? And wait...marry my sister? Oh boy! A gunslinger for my brother! Will you teach me all you know?"

"Nicholas," Winnie said, her hands on her hips.

"He's got moves with a knife." Gavin shrugged. "And that same Anderson fire his sisters have. Better he learn to take care of himself from someone who can teach him right."

Winnie groaned. He was correct, but her brother was staring at Gavin with something akin to adoration in his eyes. She glanced at Lily, and her sister was doing the same.

"Oh Winnie! Isn't that wonderful? A sheriff as my brother-in-law! We'll be so safe," Lily said. "And do you see his friends? So handsome," she sighed. "Maybe he has a few more friends my age."

Another groan escaped Winnie, but then also a laugh. Gavin moved toward her, then took her hand and led her a few steps away. Winnie saw Nick start to follow them, but Lily said something and pulled him back. Gavin's friends started to talk to her brother and sister, moving them a short distance away from the forming crowd outside the saloon.

When they were not within earshot, Gavin looked at her. "So, how about it?"

"How about what?" Winnie asked.

"Marry me. For real."

Winnie was surprised to see uncertainty in his face. He looked...nervous.

"You want to marry me?" Winnie asked. She glanced back at Lily and Nick. "I'm a package deal," she warned.

"I know it," Gavin said, tucking his thumbs into his gun belt. "That's okay by me. I've been alone most of my life. Eli and Billy were the first family I've ever had. I know what it feels like to be on your own. I also know, as a kid," he nodded to Nick and Lily, "you need to feel secure. Have someone to look after you. I'd like to be that for them. And I'd like to be the man that you love. The one who takes care of you. I understand if I'm not who you want to do that, though."

Winnie reached out and took his hand. She stared at their joined fingers, almost unsure what to say. Finally, she said, "I can't believe you want to marry me," she said. "Really marry me. I thought you were just saying it. You really want me? Lily and Nick too?" She bit her lip, hoping that this all wasn't some terrible joke or heat of the moment offer.

"Oh, Winnie, I've known it from almost the moment I laid eyes on you," Gavin said, his voice full of emotion. He pulled her into his arms. "If you say yes, I will spend every moment of the rest of my life trying to make you happy. I'll love and protect you, same with the kids. I've got a big house. They can each have their own room. We'll give them everything they need. I'll give you everything you need or could possibly want."

Gavin ran a thumb over her cheek. His eyes burned with an intensity she never thought she'd see a man have while looking at her. Winnie could hardly believe her ears. Yet...his words and the way she felt right now were perfect. They were all she wanted. She was done missing chances. Today had taught her there was too much risk in not telling someone how you felt. Winnie knew she wouldn't make that mistake again.

She smiled up at him. "Yes," she said softly. Then, she raised herself up slightly on her toes and kissed him. This kiss was different from their first. It was better. The world stopped for a moment, then everything spun around in her stomach and head, and she knew she'd given the right answer. There was nothing she wanted more than to be with Gavin for the rest of her life.

As they separated, Winnie searched his face. "You are sure? Last chance to back out. We Andersons seem a troublesome lot."

Gavin grinned and looked down at her. "Oh, I'm sure. I like trouble. Makes things interesting. Besides, I get the better end of the deal. I get you. You have to put up with a gunslinger trying to be a sheriff who doesn't always follow the rules."

"I really wouldn't have it any other way," Winnie said, lacing her fingers in his. They started to walk back to Lily and Nick, who were grinning at them. "But you're not just a gunslinger trying to be a sheriff," she said, smiling up at him. "You're mine. So don't you forget it, Gavin Jefferson."

Epilogue

Gavin played Billy's favorite song on his violin, tapping his foot in tune as he took in the scene before him. They'd finished dinner, and everyone was spread out on Billy and Mirabelle's large porch. Eli had his feet up and eyes closed. Billy was showing Lily and Nick a dance that many in the town were doing.

Hannah and Mirabelle had fast become friends with Winnie. The three of them were making plans for the new dresses they planned to make for Mirabelle's longtime friend Callie's wedding.

He and Winnie had married the day after they got back in town. Pastor Blackstone had smiled so big the whole time. Right away, they had settled in at his house—correction, his and Winnie's house—and Lily and Nick had made themselves right at home.

It had been good for Winnie to have her family there. She still struggled with a terrible guilt over her siblings' suffering, and the detective being murdered. Gavin hoped with time, some of that would ease.

With some help from a few other lawmen, they'd discovered the place posing as an orphanage really wasn't. It pretended to be one in order to sell the children for whatever purpose a buyer wanted. How Winnie had managed to leave without being sold was nothing short of a miracle.

Once the law and a judge got involved, the rest of the children had been placed either with good families, or in real orphanages, like the one his former gambling friend owned. There, the kids would get a real chance in life, and be educated and protected.

Luckily, Lily and Nick were doing just fine, and making friends as though they'd always been a part of Red Ridge.

Eli and Billy had taken right away to the kids as well, and had asked Winnie if she'd let them teach the boy how to ranch. Nick had eagerly accepted when she asked him, since part of the skills he would be learning was to rope, shoot, and defend himself against rustlers.

Lily had asked if she could perhaps continue her education that had been taken away from her at a young age. She'd always had a passion for teaching others, and Winnie had promptly agreed that was a good idea. There was a school in Red Ridge, but the teacher was quite old and looking to leave soon. Lily might make a fine replacement one day.

Billy walked over and flopped down next to Gavin. "Phew. They're wearing me out."

Gavin chuckled as he continued to play. Lily and Nick were trying the dance still, and their faces were flushed while their eyes were shining with happiness.

"Makes me glad to see them doing so well," Eli said.

"Same," Gavin answered.

"Guess who's visiting?" Billy asked.

"Oh yes!" Mirabelle gasped. "Winnie! I can't wait for you to meet her!"

"Who?" Winnie asked.

"My sister Nora," Billy said. "She's a year older than me. Got the letter today she's going to come visit for a while."

"You know who else I can't wait to see?" Hannah asked. "Whoever Gus's mysterious woman is." She glanced toward the old man, who was dancing with her young daughter, Meg. "He looks for every opportunity to run errands and go into town. But I can't get out of him who she is or where she works!"

"Guess we'll find out eventually," Eli said. He reached for Hannah's hand. "Town's not so big we won't figure it out."

The song ended, and Gavin lowered the violin. "My fingers need a break," he called to the dancers.

Winnie moved close to him and rested her head on his shoulder. "I'm so happy here," she said with a sigh. "With you, your friends, my siblings. It's like we are one large family, and it's wonderful."

"I agree," Gavin said, wrapping his arm around her.

"You know, after that excitement, I suspect we're due for a quiet spell," Billy said.

"Maybe," Eli said. He shrugged.

"Regardless of what happens, one thing's for sure," Gavin remarked, as he stared up at the night sky where the stars were just starting to emerge. "Red Ridge is going to be just fine as long as we are here."

What's next?

Find out what happens when Nora visits Red Ridge and the gunslingers are faced with a foe they can't stop.
Book 4: The Doctor
https://www.amazon.com/dp/B0DQ7HFQ15

***

And if you haven't already, be sure to get your FREE book in the Red Ridge Chronicles right here:
https://dl.bookfunnel.com/dt01yp1w38

***

Want to read (or listen!) to James and Grace's story and meet another of the gunslingers' friends? Find *A Gunslinger for Grace* right here: https://www.amazon.com/Gunslinger-Grace-Sarah-Lamb-ebook/dp/B0C5FT56DN

***

Want to meet Kody, a former gambler who spends his days fiercely protecting children at the orphanage he opened, and the teacher who thinks he's anything but honest? https://www.amazon.com/Mail-Order-Gambler-Husbands-Sarah-Lamb-ebook/dp/B0D7FWMLDP

Read all the Red Ridge Chronicles Books

https://www.amazon.com/dp/B0DQ7HFQ15

Book 1
The Gunslinger
Book 2
The Drifter

Book 3

The Lawman

Book 4

The Doctor

Book 5

The Tracker

Book 6

The Newcomer

Book 7

The Old Man

Book 8

The Christmas Wedding

Note from Author

Thank you for taking the time to read *The Lawman*. Could I ask for one small favor? Reviews like yours on Amazon mean so much to me and help others to find my books! Even just a single line means a lot!

Also...

Want a FREE book?

Stop by my website to get your no strings attached **FREE book**. It's my gift to you, as a thank you for reading this one.

www.sarahlambbooks.com

About Author

Sarah Lamb is the mother of two boys and wife to a teacher. She spends her days writing and editing books in the beautiful Shenandoah Valley.

Made in United States
Troutdale, OR
09/12/2025

34470145R00100